NANCY DREW™
The Curse

NANCY
DREW ™
The Curse

BY MICOL OSTOW

BASED ON CHARACTERS CREATED BY CAROLYN KEENE
AND
CHARACTERS FROM THE TELEVISION SERIES DEVELOPED
BY NOGA LANDAU, STEPHANIE SAVAGE & JOSH SCHWARTZ

SIMON PULSE
NEW YORK LONDON TORONTO SYDNEY NEW DELHI

This book is a work of fiction. Any references to historical events,
real people, or real places are used fictitiously. Other names, characters, places,
and events are products of the author's imagination, and any resemblance to
actual events or places or persons, living or dead, is entirely coincidental.

SIMON PULSE
An imprint of Simon & Schuster Children's Publishing Division
1230 Avenue of the Americas, New York, New York 10020
First Simon Pulse hardcover edition March 2020
Nancy Drew TM & © 2020 by CBS Studios Inc. All Rights Reserved.
Text by Micol Ostow
Jacket illustration by Martin Ansin
For information about special discounts for bulk purchases, please contact
Simon & Schuster Special Sales at 1-866-506-1949 or business@simonandschuster.com.
The Simon & Schuster Speakers Bureau can bring authors to your live event.
For more information or to book an event contact the Simon & Schuster Speakers
Bureau at 1-866-248-3049 or visit our website at www.simonspeakers.com.
Jacket designed by Sarah Creech
Interior designed by Tom Daly
The text of this book was set in Adobe Garamond Pro.
Manufactured in the United States of America
2 4 6 8 10 9 7 5 3 1
Library of Congress Control Number 2019956513
ISBN 978-1-5344-7074-3 (hc)
ISBN 978-1-5344-7076-7 (eBook)

NANCY DREW™
The Curse

PROLOGUE

I'm someone who likes to question what we know of as the so-called truth.

Yes, I do believe in the *myth* of the American Gothic: that small-town charm is its own form of parody, and that hometown pride is really just fear wrapped up in its shiny Sunday best. I believe Norman Rockwell and Grant Wood both would have had a field day with the chance to paint a pastoral scene of my hometown, Horseshoe Bay. But what would they have seen of us, if they'd turned to our own coastal dreamland as their muse?

Peel back the veneer of any charming American small town, and you're bound to uncover the black, rotting heart that lurks beneath.

I've lived in Horseshoe Bay my whole life. Its rituals, its traditions—they're mine, as ingrained into me as fingerprints, infused into my DNA.

And I do love life here, small-town secrets notwithstanding. I love the real, live things, the tiny quirks and little details that bring our town to light, to life. Like the annual Horseshoe Bay Naming Day Festival, reliable as the equinox, perennial as the spring's lengthening daylight. A celebration of our roots and our history as a community.

After all: What could be more festive?

My own favorite Naming Day memories are drenched in icy lemonade and soaked in the crisp, sunny air of spring. They smell of the season's last lingering evening fire and the glow of starlight as the sun slips down past the horizon line. I remember things: being impossibly small, watching as a court of older girls, sylphlike, swans, glided by, flower crowns twined through their hair and trailing in the blue hush of dusk. I remember the sound of my mother's voice—off-key, filled with laughter—as she sang along to our favorite Horseshoe Bay hits, performed live (and also off-key; that was practically a rule) in the town's tiny band shell. And when I was younger still, I remember cornhole and Ferris wheel rides, painted-face mermaid queens, holding hands with childhood friends as our bucket crested the machine's highest curve, mouths stretched in delighted terror.

But I'm not the only one with Naming Day memories. Everyone in this town has their own.

And legend has it, some of them are far from happy.

Too bad I don't believe in legends. Just like I don't believe in black magic, or the paranormal, or anything beyond what I can see with my own two eyes.

Blood. Science. Facts. These are the things I believe in. Things that I can quantify. Things that I can prove, that I can hold in my hand.

I believe in small towns, salty air, and, yes, even the dark secrets that my friends and neighbors carry with them, close to their hearts. We all have our own skeletons, our own crosses to bear. That's just a fact, a by-product of basic human nature.

But legends? Tall tales? Curses?

No.

A curse is just a mystery dressed up in a sharp, stern warning. I don't believe in curses.

But everyone knows that I love a mystery.

And everyone knows a mystery doesn't stand a chance next to me.

PART ONE

THE FESTIVAL

CHAPTER ONE

Friday

Countdown to the Naming Day Cast List Is OVER

If there's one thing the good people of
Horseshoe Bay love, it's a celebration, and
maybe none more than the annual Naming
Day Festival! And the jewel in the crown of the
two-day celebration? Well, people may debate
their own favorites—and do they ever!—but it's
safe to say that the Naming Day live naming
reenactment, held on Saturday afternoon, is
always a strong contender.

This year, expectations and enthusiasm
are at an all-time high, as we all get ready for
the seventy-fifth anniversary of the naming of
our fair town. After all, what could be more
jubilant than a Horseshoe Bay jubilee?

So it's no wonder, then, that the halls of

Keene High have been buzzing with excitement and *lots* of speculation about who the lucky cast members of this year's show will be. Fear not, fellow Neptunes! Sources have revealed that the full cast list is set to go up in the quad this afternoon, and will be waiting for all of you dying-to-get-the-deets folks by the chime of final bell today. You heard it here first! Now get thee to the quad and keep those fingers crossed. For a few lucky seniors, this Naming Day Festival is set to be their best yet!

"Wow, Nancy, that's definitely a . . . *perky* piece you have in today's *Masthead*. Seriously, I'm exhausted just from *skimming* it. Did you accidentally inhale some cold medicine this morning?"

I closed my locker door to find Lena Barrow, head cheerleader and one-third of my utterly inseparable high school trio, waiting for me with a bemused grin on her lips and a folded-up copy of the latest issue of the school paper—replete with my own latest byline—in her hands.

"Oh, really?" I rolled my eyes at her. Lena was no stranger to strong opinions—and she *wasn't* shy about voicing them, which meant that she sometimes had a tendency to strike terror in the hearts of her fellow classmates. Lucky for me, I understood Lena, "got" that her bark was worse than her bite. Luckier still, I don't scare easily. "Noted."

"What are we noting?"

Speaking of "perky," right on cue, there was Daisy Dewitt, the third in our power trifecta, hovering at Lena's side and practically thrumming with energy. Her wide, blue eyes sparkled, and even her shiny, sun-streaked blond hair radiated excitement. Lena may have been our head cheerleader, but Daisy was definitely MVP when it came to team spirit. And generally speaking, she was a kinder, softer cool girl than our queen bee. And she was my best friend.

"Only the fact that the festival is officially here!" I squeezed her hand. Daisy was a senior, which meant this was her year to—hopefully—snag top billing in the annual reenactment. Girl was a shoo-in for various reasons; her last name alone conferred on her "founding family" status, which was as close as Horseshoe Bay got to royalty. But, adorably, she still managed to be nervous about the whole thing. And her humility wasn't even fake. Which made what would have been downright insufferable on anyone else completely charming on her. It's one of my favorite things about her, and a big part of why we've been friends since our preschool days.

"The festival *cast list*, to be specific," she said. "As profiled so deftly in your actually rather, uh, enthusiastic *Masthead* piece."

Lena waggled an eyebrow, smug. "What did I tell you, Nance? I'm just saying, it was the punctuation."

"Guys, I get it. I promise, next time I'll go lighter on the exclamation marks." To be honest, I'd been iffy on them. Anyway, "perky" isn't usually my thing.

Daisy linked an arm through each of ours and began leading

us down the hall at a rather brisk pace. "It's okay," she trilled. "I know you were just excited for Naming Day—meaning, for *me*. You guys are probably the only two people as excited for me as I am!" She giggled. Sometimes hanging out with Daisy felt like being shaken up inside a giant bottle of soda, bubbling and sweet and threatening at any moment to froth up and totally spill over the rim. But in a good way.

We passed down the hall through the back exit of the school, which led outside to the wide, grassy expanse of the quad. The sky was marbled blue, shot through with milky swirls of cloud, and the quad itself was . . .

Lena was the first to say it. "Yikes. There will be blood."

"It's definitely looking a little *Hunger Games* out here," I agreed. A slight exaggeration—but only just. The quad was wall-to-wall Neptunes, seniors clamoring for a peek at the Naming Day cast list while their friends lingered in the background.

"How did all these people get outside before we did?" Daisy moaned. "I came straight to you guys after final bell."

"That was your first mistake," Lena said.

"Ugh, I'm going in." She threw a quick wave at us over her shoulder and dashed off to maneuver her way through the fray, a crush of students clustered around the giant oak tree where announcements were traditionally posted.

I watched, proud, as Daisy hip-checked another senior girl, offering up her best "shy," apologetic smile. "Well, she definitely did *not* come to play." This was a big moment for her, and her enthusiasm was infectious.

"My little girl's growing up," Lena said, wiping a mock tear from her cheek, even though Lena was in my grade and therefore younger than Daisy. "Seriously, though, can you blame her? She comes from a *founding family*. This is, like, the role she was born for. She's been counting down to this Naming Day since we were still in diapers."

It was the truth. Daisy came from a long line of Dewitts, aka one of the actual, original founding families that the Naming Day Festival commemorated each year. It was one of her great-great-great- (etc. and so on) grandfathers who'd signed the original Horseshoe Bay town charter. Colonel Chester Dewitt, a war hero, no less—his was one of the most coveted roles in the yearly reenactment, in point of fact. Every year, the ceremony staged a grand reenactment of some of the earliest highlights of life in Horseshoe Bay, culminating in a rendition of the original naming ceremony itself. Of course, Daisy's family was too genteel to fall back on anything so gauche as nepotism, so when it came to nabbing her own starring role in the reenactment, Daisy had had to wait until senior year just like everyone else to be eligible to audition.

At least, that was my take. The truth was, the Dewitts were a bit . . . eccentric. And part of their eccentricity meant that they liked to keep down low and out of sight. Sometimes to an extreme length.

Her family was huge, aunts and uncles and cousins flowering in every direction like a family tree gone climbing ivy. But other than Daisy, they preferred to live on the outskirts of town, children being homeschooled and parents preferring each other's company to that of anyone else in town. "Odd" was how my parents described the Dewitts, generously. "Cultish freaks" was another phrase that came up among less enlightened people in the town.

Their self-imposed seclusion meant none of us knew her family or her parents well, not even those of us who were close to her. Daisy had begged her parents to let her go to the public high school—and waged another battle, freshman year, when she'd negotiated with them to try out for cheerleading—but the Dewitts kept to themselves. Sleepovers were strictly Lena's or my domain, for example. Just one more reason I was so excited for her to have her shining Naming Day moment—her parents' protectiveness extended to extracurriculars, and she'd missed a few, over time.

Suddenly, a thought occurred to me. "There's no chance she *won't* get cast, right? And . . . her parents will let her perform?" I asked Lena. On the one hand, I believed it. On the other hand, if I was wrong? It was going to be ugly. Even if only based on the competition-reality-TV-esque scenario currently playing out on my high school's quad.

Lena looked at me. "Not possible she wouldn't get cast. Our girl's got the pedigree, and you know her audition was rock-solid. No way her parents would take that away from her."

I appreciated Lena's faith, but being in my line of work, I knew that people could surprise you.

As for Daisy's audition, she was right. There was no doubt

about that. Daisy was big into Drama Club, and had been the lead in every school play since fifth grade. (One of the few times a year we'd see her extended family was when they'd trundle out to see her perform.) I was sure her Naming Day audition was flawless.

"Even putting aside her acting skills, her family must do their own personal staging of the Naming Ceremony at, like, Thanksgiving dinners, right? At least, that's how I always pictured their holidays. Daisy has to know the whole script by h— oh, wait, here we go," Lena said, leaning into me so close our shoulders briefly brushed. "She made it to the front of the mob. She's at the cast list . . . she's looking at the list, searching for her name . . . searching . . . searching . . ."

"It's like we're on safari, watching the animals tear one another apart. Except less civilized. People know this is a *town play*, right?"

I loved Horseshoe Bay, sure, but sometimes it still made me laugh, watching people get so invested in small-town hijinks that they'd practically shiv a classmate to grab the first look at a cast list. The thing about a small town? It is, by definition, *small*. I could tell you my classmates' full names and who they were named after, and who had a nut allergy, and who was faking some unnamed physical condition to get out of gym class. I personally had my sights set on bigger things, broader horizons, greener pastures. The stuff of motivational posters in guidance counselors' offices everywhere.

"Yes, yes, we all know *you've* got one foot out the door, Nancy

Drew," Lena teased. "But I'll remind you of this moment next year, when we're both fully tripping each other, sprinting, trying to be the first one to the cast list. It's easy to be low-key about it when we're both still juniors. But you and I both know that down deep, you're as much of a sucker for Horseshoe Bay and all its kitschy, nostalgia-soaked glory as anyone else."

I opened my mouth to reply—mostly just to agree with her—but before I could say a word, I was tackled by a giant mass of soda-fizz glee and blond hair.

"I got it!" Daisy shrieked. "I got the part! Abigail Dewitt, the settler who fed the town through the coldest winter on record, even after she was partially blinded from scarlet fever."

"Are you sure that was Abigail Dewitt, and not a scene from the Little House on the Prairie books?" I teased as I hugged her back. "Congratulations, though, really."

"Abigail Dewitt, huh?" Lena joked. "Feels a little bit like typecasting, TBH."

Daisy waved her off. "It's not the biggest part in the reenactment, but it's definitely the best. It's a whole new scene they added—"

"—*in honor of the jubilee celebration*," Lena and I chimed in, laughing.

"And Coop got Jebediah Dewitt, *so* . . ." She trailed off, one eyebrow perfectly arched. Cooper Smith was captain of the football team, which, according to the unflinching rules of adolescent clichés, meant that he was one of the most sought-after guys on campus. But unfortunately for the rest of the school, he only had eyes for Daisy. We knew better than to ask how she'd gotten her parents to let her *date*. To love Daisy—like we did—was to accept her curious—and curiously secretive—family.

"You guys must be psyched," Lena said. "Does he get to apply cold compresses to your fevered forehead onstage? Or bandage your gangrene-infected leg?"

"Ew." Daisy's tiny mouth puckered in distaste. "I'm ignoring you. Anyway, you don't need to be jealous. It's going to be you two next year!"

"The anticipation is killing me," Lena said, but she was smiling anyway. Even this year, there was plenty for us to get involved in. We were already knee-deep in every volunteer committee. It was just what you did in our town.

Case in point: The throngs of students swarming, clawing their way toward the cast list, had begun to disperse, evolving into triumphant cries as people found their own names. Amanda Reeser, who I'd helped in middle school when she suspected someone was sabotaging her science fair project (they were), was doing a little happy dance that left no room for misinterpretation. Competitive as it was, since the reenactment spots were reserved for seniors, almost everyone who auditioned was given *some* role, so the energy on the quad was happy and bright. It was infectious; Daisy's Naming Day was my Naming Day, *our* Naming Day, and yes, Lena would have rolled her eyes so hard they'd pop out of their sockets if she heard me going all mushy. But regardless: Mushy was how I felt. My friends were happy. I was happy. All was unusually peaceful and well.

Daisy led us back across the quad, now that people were clustering up, exchanging teary, excited hugs and high fives with friends, and chattering about lines, costumes, rehearsals, and other *let's all get ready* kinds of things. It was like a mine-field, but of shining, grinning teenagers, instead of anything dangerous.

Well, instead of anything *truly* dangerous, that is. We were an energy drink commercial just waiting to happen.

"I can't *believe* this!"

I stopped in my tracks, just a moment before Daisy and Lena caught on to what was going down.

There it was: the land mine.

At the top of the quad, right next to the oak tree with its cast list flapping in the afternoon breeze, stood Caroline Mark. I didn't know her that well—we'd had AP Bio together for a semester when she moved to Horseshoe Bay; she wasn't a natural when it came to dissections—but I didn't have to know her well to read the expression on her face just then.

Though the day was flawless and sunny, her face was a stone-cold thundercloud. Even from where we stood in the middle of the lawn, I could see her brown eyes glittering with outright fury. Her cheeks were red, and I could just make out a slight sheen of sweat on her brow.

I'm an investigative journalist; I notice details.

"Caroline . . ." It was Anna Gardner, a friend of hers, clearly. Anna was doing her best to calm Caroline, but it was like trying

to Scotch tape the window shades down during a hurricane.
Totally pointless.

"*Don't* tell me to calm down!" she snarled. She ripped the
cast list down from the tree and began tearing it into tiny pieces,
her movements frantic. Students who'd been clustered around,
observing with anxious curiosity, moved back, giving her a wide
berth and a *lot* of cautious side-eye.

Lena inhaled sharply. "Whaaat is happening?" She sounded
curious—but still slightly thrilled—at the drama we were watching unravel. If Lena's favorite thing was *causing* drama, then her
second favorite was standing back to observe as it unfolded. I
was less eager to watch this very public breakdown.

Daisy grabbed my arm, tight enough that for a second I worried she'd leave a bruise. "OMG, that's Caroline Mark—you know
her," she said, her voice low, as though Caroline might actually hear
us from halfway across the lawn through the throes of her epic
meltdown-in-progress. "She's in Drama Club, but, like, she's new."

"Oh, yeah," Lena said. "Weird that I barely recognize her. A
tantrum like this feels like something I'd remember."

"I've seen her around," I said. "She's usually less . . . scream-y.
I think." Although if memory served, she'd been pretty out-
spoken about the dissection thing.

"She is," Daisy confirmed. "But like I said, she's new enough
to Drama Club, and, like, doesn't get that there's, you know, a
hierarchy to these things. I mean, I think she just expected to
march in on the first day of the semester and get picked for the
lead in the school musical."

"There's a school musical?" Lena joked. As if anyone could forget; we'd been coming to Daisy's performances since what felt like the dawn of time.

"It's *Little Shop of Horrors* this year, remember?!" Daisy snapped hastily. "I'm Audrey, of course. The woman Audrey, not the plant. The plant is technically Audrey Two. But *anyway*. So Caroline just . . . like, *waltzed* in and was all, *I took vocal coaching over the summer; you should hear my mezzo soprano* . . . and the drama coach was not impressed."

"Because there's a hierarchy," Lena said.

"Exactly. And she tried out for Naming Day because, you know, she's a senior, so she has—"

"Seniority—" I put in helpfully.

"*Exactly!*" she said, happy.

"But I'm guessing she didn't get cast," Lena said drily.

Up at the front of the quad, poor Caroline Mark was flinging her thousands of tiny bits of paper into her hapless friend's face, still shrieking at top volume and flailing *very* dramatically.

"If she did, she's taking it really weird," Daisy said. "It's so awkward."

"And yet I can't look away," Lena breathed. "God, I do so love petty high school drama."

That makes one of us. I had to say something. "Okay, you guys, this voyeurism thing is starting to make me feel bad. We don't need to stick around and watch this." Caroline's pain was a little too raw, and I wasn't Lena; watching it triggered my sympathy bone, big-time. True, I hung with the "cool kids," but solving mysteries didn't always win me popularity points. I knew what it felt like to be an outsider. And I only eavesdrop when strictly necessary.

Which still happens to be quite often, but that was beside the point.

"Speak for yourself," Lena said.

"Anyway, look—she's going to be fine," Daisy said, pointing. We followed her gaze to see the English teacher, Mr. Stephenson, who dabbled as the drama teacher, come rushing out the back door to where Caroline was still spinning out. Gently, he rested a hand on her shoulder and leaned in.

He whispered something into her ear, and I watched as, slowly, the fire in her eyes ebbed to a dull spark. She didn't look less angry, per se—only slightly calmer. She said something to him in return—something impassioned, based on her body language and wild gesticulations. But her shoulders were beginning to slump now, and it was obvious that the edge was beginning to ebb from her fight.

"Show's over, I guess," Lena said, sounding disappointed. "What now? There's been way too much excitement for us to just go home."

"The Claw?" Daisy suggested. "I think Coop said some of the other seniors are going to stop by to celebrate. But even if they don't, we still can. I don't have to be home for a while. I told Mom and Dad I had tutoring after school." She gave a little excited shimmy with her shoulders.

"An excellent plan," Lena said. "You know I'm always up for a lobster roll."

I heard their exchange, but it was distant and muddled, wavering in the background like a soundtrack. I was distracted as I observed Mr. Stephenson shepherd a definitely still-disgruntled Caroline back into the school building, her arms folded defiantly across her chest. He'd slung one arm over her shoulder and was giving her a comforting squeeze. A little more snuggly than most teachers might get with a student, but it did seem to be calming Caroline down.

"Earth to Nancy," Lena said, her voice breaking into my thoughts at last—though just barely. "Fries? Lobster rolls?"

"Sure," I murmured, still only half listening.

The truth was, Caroline's little demonstration had definitely caught my eye. No matter how worked up our town gets over its rituals and celebrations, her response to being left off the cast list of the Naming Day reenactment was . . . intense. It didn't strike me as the reaction of a well-balanced person.

And the way that Stephenson's arm was draped across her shoulders? That, too, got my Spidey Sense tingling.

And the look on Caroline's face, now, as she moved back into the building? It wasn't the look of a girl who'd come to terms with some disappointing news. Nor was it the face of someone who'd been placated well enough, cozy half hugs from drama coaches notwithstanding.

No, Caroline Mark stalked into the high school now looking grimly determined, by my estimation. Like someone who wouldn't easily forget how badly she'd been wronged or slighted.

Like someone who was, maybe, just barely holding her tongue, and biding her time.

CHAPTER TWO

W hoa," Daisy said as we pulled into the parking lot of the Claw. "Coop said he was gonna swing by with some of the seniors. Not, like, the entire senior class."

"Semantics, obviously," Lena said, waving a hand.

It turned out, the lot was almost more crowded with cars than the quad had been with students after school, and we found ourselves squeezing Daisy's bright blue Mini into the last available spot. Thank God my girl was way too invested in aesthetics to drive anything as practical as a four-door, or we'd never have made it in.

"I'm not sure this is actually a spot," Lena said, craning toward us from the tiny back seat so her face hovered just between ours.

"Fire lanes are just suggestions. Look, the water is *right there*." Daisy pointed toward the pebbled trail leading from the parking lot to the rocky bluff beyond. "In the highly unlikely event of a fire, we are all good."

"I . . . don't think that's how fire safety works, Daisy," I said. And I wasn't sure I'd be able to open the door to get out on my own side either. But Daisy obviously wasn't worried about it; she was already killing the ignition and humming to herself as she cracked her own door open—extremely carefully—and shimmied sideways to ease herself out.

Lena grumbled, sliding along the bench of the back seat and sucking her stomach in as much as she could, exhaling only after she'd maneuvered her way around the car and into slightly more open space. She flashed me a sarcastic thumbs-up. "You got this, Nancy."

Choosing the coveted shotgun seat had clearly been a major mistake. But somehow I managed my own way out of the car without injuring myself, and soon we were making our way through the front door of the diner. A tiny bell echoed as it slammed back shut against its frame behind us. The scent—salt and brine and the lingering tang of happy hours past—enveloped us, along with the heat of a tightly packed space.

"I see the theme of the day is: overpopulation," Lena observed, not incorrectly. Inside, the Claw was at full capacity, the atmosphere celebratory and happy, as opposed to the meltdown we witnessed back at the quad. "Are we even going to be able to get a booth?"

"Daisy!" From a table far in the back, Cooper beckoned, his face lit up. "You made it! I saved you a seat!" He gestured to a tiny sliver of space beside himself that absolutely did not look person-size at all.

She glanced at us, giving a quick flash of puppy-dog eyes. "You guys don't mind, do you?"

"What, being left behind as you join the royal court to bask in all your reenactment glory? No, we don't mind at all," Lena quipped. "Feel free to abandon your besties at will. For a boy that is basically the human equivalent of a Labrador retriever, no less."

"Settle down," Daisy said. "I know you think basic niceness is some kind of mortal weakness, but Coop's a good guy. There's nothing wrong with that."

Lena shrugged. "High school is survival of the fittest, that's all."

I gave Lena a little nudge. "And Cooper is nothing if not fit." To Daisy, I offered, "Of course we don't. Go say hi. We'll"—I looked around, considering our limited options—"grab a seat at the counter." The counter, a long stretch of well-worn wood draped in nautically thematic décor like fishing nets and anchors, was prime real estate for nursing a soda and people-watching, anyway. It wasn't a huge sacrifice.

"Or I can scare those scabby-looking JV girls out of that booth over there," Lena said, pointing. I waved her off, not bothering to dignify the comment with a response. Even if her bark was worse than her bite, sometimes a loud bark was a lot all on its own.

"Cool," Daisy said, looking relieved. "I'll just, like, check in with Coop and stuff, and then I'll be back, and we can have girl time."

"You'll be back. Suuure," Lena said. I gave her another sharp poke to the ribs, and she yelped. "I'm just messing with you. Take your time. Enjoy. Bask away. Just don't forget you're our ride home."

Daisy assumed a solemn expression. "I would never. Cross my heart and hope to . . . have the lead role in the Naming Day reenactment taken away."

I widened my eyes. "Heresy!" If I'd believed in jinxes, I'd have warned her against jinxing herself. But I never bothered with those, even as a little kid.

"Fanciful" was not a word people typically used to describe Nancy Drew.

With a smile, Daisy flounced off to Cooper's waiting sliver of booth, and Lena and I were left to weave our way to the two remaining seats at the counter, back in the farthest corner of the space. From our perch, we could see through the pass-through to the kitchen, where the staff was obviously having a hard time keeping up with the oversize after-school crowd's appetite. I wasn't necessarily *trying* to eavesdrop—like I said, I'm just naturally observant—but the acoustics of the space and the way my stool was positioned meant that it was harder *not* to listen in to the kitchen's panicky conversation than anything going on in the overstuffed dining room. And I *definitely* wasn't *not* trying to eavesdrop, per se.

"You've *got* to pick up the pace, Ace," someone was saying. She was facing away from me so that all I could see were twin braids down her back, glossy and sleek as licorice whips. For his part, Ace—the dishwasher, a newer addition to the Claw's staff—swathed in a soaked and food-stained apron and elbow-length rubber gloves, grudgingly eyed a plastic bin filled to over-flowing with dishware that rested on a metal rolling rack beside him. His hair, a shaggy-cut sandy-brown, flopped over one eye, curling up slightly in the humidity of the small space.

If he was stressed about being reprimanded, it didn't show. "We're in the weeds, George," he said, shrugging. "It just means business is booming. That's a good thing. Be . . . grateful?"

"I'll be grateful when you can actually keep up with the bare minimum requirements of your job," she snapped, turning so I could see the rigid set of her jaw and the stony look in her dark eyes.

George Fan. We'd been close when we were little—we'd even taken some Ferris wheel rides together at some long-ago Naming Days. But we barely crossed paths anymore. Which was, I think we'd both agree, by design. Did I ever think about how we used to be so close, back before middle school, cliques, exclusive and exclusionary birthday parties, rumors, notes passed, nasty online comments?

Nope. Definitely not. The past was the past, and George had made it abundantly clear there was no changing it. So why dwell? According to her, I'd defected from our friendship as soon as I'd started hanging with Lena and her crew—that loud bark of Lena's had burned more than a few bridges, George's being one of them.

That didn't mean it didn't hurt to see her.

I knew she worked at the Claw; it was the obvious after-school gig for a high schooler with an . . . unreliable home situation. But even though it was the default hangout for basically anyone in town with a pulse, I'd managed to avoid overlapping my visits with her shifts.

Until now.

Or maybe not "somehow." Maybe, knowing George, that was by design too.

"In case you hadn't noticed, Ace," she was saying now, "this crowd is kinda atypical for us. Business in this place *isn't* exactly booming, most of the time. Meaning, it's up to us to hustle on the rare occasions that it picks up." She narrowed her eyes, lowered her voice, and adopted a hands-on-hips power stance. *"Like today."* She balled up a dish towel and launched it at him, pivoting sharply on one heel to make her way back into the dining room.

As she moved toward my corner of the counter, I straightened, trying to look as though I'd been doing anything other than fully stalking her not-so-inspirational behind-the-scenes pep talk.

"Relax, Drew," she snapped, catching my eye as she stalked past me. "I know you heard all that."

"People in *Canada* heard that," Lena sniped. "If you were looking to keep it on the DL, next time think about lowering your voice."

"I wasn't . . . ," I started, but quickly trailed off because, let's be real: I totally *was*. "Sorry. It, uh, looks like you've got your hands full."

"Don't worry," she said, sneering, "no one's looking at you to apply. Nobody would expect *Nancy Drew* to give up her perfect college-bound dreams to come work at a dive like this."

"I—didn't—" I protested.

"What is your problem, Fan?" Lena cut in. "Like it's our fault that you and your staff are having loud fights in front of the customers?"

"It's okay," I said, reaching out a hand to Lena, but she waved me off.

"Just because you and Nancy hung out, like, once upon a time, doesn't mean she owes you anything now."

George narrowed her eyes at Lena. "Thanks for clarifying." Then she looked at me. "But if you're waiting for someone to take your order, I'd settle in and get *real* patient, if I were you."

I met her gaze. "Understood," I said, a mix of emotions flooding through me as she moved off, leaving Lena and me with our still-unopened menus spread on the counter in front of us.

"God, she is *such* a freak," Lena said, leaning her head toward me but not bothering to lower her voice. "It's funny you guys used to hang out." She gave a "playful" wave at George, off at the other end of the bar wiping down some glasses. She noted the wave and glared fiercely at the both of us.

Yeah. *Funny.* I bit back an impulse to defend George, but I wasn't totally sure why.

"Sunny as ever," Lena said, watching George's retreating body, marching past us still ramrod straight. "Good thing we haven't ordered anything, or I'd say she's *definitely* spitting in your drink."

"Stop," I said. "She's . . ." But I couldn't figure out how to end the sentence, or how to articulate everything that immediately crossed my mind when George got bitchy or gave me attitude—which was pretty much whenever she saw me, these days.

"Never mind." I looked at the battered, laminated menus resting on the counter beside us. "I'm *hungry*," I realized. Not that I needed a menu—cheese fries all the way.

"Yeah, well, based on the little performance George just put on, we'll be lucky to get our orders in this century. Which is a real pity, as we're going to need all our strength about us in the coming days."

I had to laugh at that. "You sound like a general rallying the troops."

"I kind of am," Lena said. "But there's a ton for us to do, even if we're mere peons when it comes to the actual marquee event."

"I prefer to think of us as active bystanders," I said.

"Whatever floats your boat," Lena said. "No pun intended."

"Speaking of—well, floats and puns," I said, "we're going to be working on Daisy's, right?" We'd already told her we would; we were going to meet in the shop studio later this week to get started. Naming Day always culminated in a grand parade on Sunday morning, and our questionable construction skills were put to the test every year.

Lena sighed dramatically. "I dimly recall a promise of that sort."

"It'll be fun!" The power of positive thinking had to count for *something*, right?

"Maybe," Lena said. "I mean, decorating is one thing—I'm

all over a tissue-paper flower wreath, and you know I'm a maniac with a hot glue gun."

"I will happily confirm your hot glue gun prowess." That was something too, right? There was a reason everyone had wanted to team up with Lena for science fair projects in grade school, and it wasn't because she was a science prodigy.

"But I think this year, we might have to actually *construct* some of the floats. Like, from wood, and nails, and . . . well, I can't think of another thing, which I think just goes to show that I'm probably the *last* person who should be given access to the power tools."

"No one's talking about power tools," I said. Although . . . there *were* an awful lot of those stored in the shop studio. "Or, at least, I hope not. But you're crafty, I'm crafty—"

"You hold your mother's pincushion while she sews the Naming Day costumes," Lena interjected. "Let's not overstate things."

"Okay, I'm *crafty-adjacent*," I said. "Whatever. But it's not like we've never, you know, *made* anything before. We can totally build a float." I tried to sound more confident than I felt. The mention of power tools had sent a small frisson of dread down my spine.

"If you say so."

"I do."

I did. I *had* to. Because Lena was right: this week was going to be full-on crazy. Daisy and the rest of the seniors would be knee-deep in the reenactment preparations, but that only meant an endless to-do list of other tasks for the rest of us. Like Lena said, my mother and I handled costumes (even if my assistance was in more of an "apprentice" capacity), and though we'd mostly gotten it down to a routine after so many Naming Days under our belt, this one promised to be different. It was the jubilee, after all, and everything was going to be ever-so-slightly dialed up.

"So you're, what—costumes and snacks? Your mom's going to do those blondies for the bay party after the show, right?" Lena was the only person more obsessed with my mom's baking than I was. Mom was famous for her strawberry blondies, which she liked to claim were an homage to my hair. Personally, I thought they were an homage to her love of baked goods.

"Try and stop her. I dare you." No one ever would. "But yes, technically the two of us will be working on that together. I'm way better with a measuring spoon than I am with a needle and thread. And you're doing the school's social media account, right?"

She made a face. "Don't remind me. I can't believe Principal Wagner tapped me for that." She narrowed her eyes at me. "Remind me why you let that happen?"

I held my hands up. "If I recall correctly, there was no stopping you."

Lena was as notoriously hooked to her phone as phones themselves were notoriously banned during school hours. Needless to say, it wasn't the greatest mix, and more often than not, Lena found herself getting called out for various phone-related infractions. Her most recent violation—updating her Twitter feed after she'd finished an English quiz early—had landed her the role as social media coordinator for Keene High's Instagram account. I had to hand it to Principal Wagner—it was a punishment rooted in pragmatism.

The irony was, not only would she be excellent at it, but she'd definitely enjoy it too. If it hadn't actually been assigned to her as a punishment, she probably would have volunteered for the job herself.

"It'll be fine," I said. "You were made for the job."

"Just like *I* was made for the role of one Abigail Dewitt!"

I looked up, startled, to see Daisy standing over us, grinning. "I literally just ate Coop's entire cheeseburger. I'm so full I'm gonna explode." She looked at our menus, still resting on the counter in front of us. "What'd you guys have? Lobster rolls?"

"Ha. That's cute," Lena said. "Please don't mock our pain."

"We, uh, actually haven't even ordered yet," I said.

"Yikes." Daisy's eyes went wide. "Sorry, you should have come over to our table. I definitely could have spared some of my burger."

"You mean Cooper's burger, right?" Lena put in. "But either way, now you tell us. When it's too late for anything to be done." She held up her phone, squinting at Daisy through the lens. "Come on. Smile and say, *My best friends are starving!*"

"My best friends are starving!" Daisy gave her most brilliant smile, which was a lot. She held out her hand to see the picture, taking the phone to look it over and giving a quick nod of approval. "You're good to post."

"It's going on the school feed," Lena said. "This will be my inaugural post as social media coordinator of the jubilee Naming Day."

"I'm honored," Daisy said. She put a hand on her stomach and frowned slightly. "And still really, really full."

Lena jabbed at the screen a few times. "Filter, filter, filter. Crop, crop, crop. There," she said finally. "You're live. Fresh as a daisy, ha ha. Now, we just sit back and let the *likes* roll in. And, of course, Nancy and I get back to the zillion other things we've got to take care of for Naming Day. It's about to get real." She looked at us.

"It's official, girls. Naming Day preparations are underway."

A horseshoe is known as a symbol of luck, but here in this crescent bay, some haven't been lucky at all. Some have found the bay itself to be less a body of tranquility and more a chasm of death and despair.

Bodies of water can give life, or they can take it.

And human bodies can sink.

Our founders have their secrets. They've done their best to bury the past, to replace trauma with revelry and to rewrite the script.

But water has memory. Sleeping dogs don't lie.

And secrets aren't secrets for long.

Would that I had power, no one in this wretched town would be given even a moment's peace. But as it is, my reach is limited, my strength finite.

How lucky, then, that this year, she should be singled out for the ceremony. I suppose the history of the horseshoe has for once worked in my favor. In our favor—mine, and those who've come before and after.

And on a jubilee year, no less!

Fate can, on occasion, be somewhat auspicious, it would seem.

She will be front and center amidst the revelry . . . and I shall be behind the scenes, waiting. Even with my limitations, it's astounding the power I can yield.

The townspeople, so simple-minded—they call it a curse.

I call it fate.

Or, in less benevolent moments, vengeance.

Call it what you will, but I shall offer this final thought:

Whatever one chooses to call it, over the years I've become expertly adept at administering it.

And this Naming Day, its vaunted jubilee year, will be no different.

CHAPTER THREE

Saturday

Nancy! Are you under that heap somewhere? What happened, did you rob the fabric store?" My father laughed as I awkwardly maneuvered myself and three times my body weight in supplies through the front door.

"If only." I dropped at my feet the two enormous bags of fabric, trim, and ostensibly anything else a person might need in order to create costumes from scratch for the entire cast of this year's jubilee Naming Day reenactment. "You wouldn't believe what I paid for all this stuff."

"I won't ask," he said, helping me move the bags from the foyer to our dining room table and gather up anything threatening to spill free. Once my hands were empty, he gave me a quick squeeze hello. "And I wouldn't venture a guess. You're doing God's work, you and your mom."

"We're doing *someone's* work," I said, eyeing the sagging bags.

"I'm not totally sure how Mom always gets roped into doing *all* the costumes for Naming Day. There's no way we're the only people in Horseshoe Bay who own a sewing machine."

"No, but your mother *is* the only person in this town who'd never hesitate to offer herself up for a task that needed doing, no matter how much it inconvenienced her to do so." There was a ring of admiration to Dad's tone that I recognized—and shared.

"Truth." I pulled out a chair and slumped into it, feeling as deflated as those two shopping bags. "Also? That crafts store on a Saturday afternoon? Not exactly the most relaxing place to be."

"I believe that, too." Dad laughed again.

I sighed. "I should find Mom and let her know I've got all the supplies and we can get started whenever she's ready." Never mind that the only thing I was ready for was a major nap.

"Actually, she's resting right now."

"Resting?" That didn't sound like my mom. Frankly, none of us Drews were all that good at just lying around.

Dad nodded. "She had a long visit to the detention center this morning. New client. I think it was pretty draining. 'Just a kid . . . wrong place, wrong time. No one on his team.' You know your mother."

"I sure do." Mom was fiercely passionate about her career as a social worker. Case in point (literally): If a new client was being detained at the juvenile detention center and needed a meeting with his caseworker, she was there, Saturday or no. And she *stayed* there for as long as her client needed her.

Dad glanced at me, no doubt processing the multitude of

microexpressions flitting across my face. "It's nothing, sweets. Everyone needs a siesta now and again. Lord knows your mother deserves one. Can you maybe do something to get started on the costumes?"

"I could cut the patterns," I said. There was no way I'd be able to handle *all* the costumes on my own, but that much, I could do. First, though: "But maybe I'll bring her a cup of tea."

"She'd appreciate that," Dad said. In the fading afternoon light, his eyes were rimmed in shadows. He seemed tired, too. *Nothing to do but keep going.* If Mom was dealing with a tough case, the best thing I could do would be to make life a little easier for her, starting with those costumes.

Monday

mean, if anyone deserves a little self-care, it's your mother, Nancy," Daisy said reproachfully. "You're usually the first person to admit that."

The final bell had just rung, signaling a blissful end to the first day back to school after the weekend. But for Daisy and me, the day was hardly over. After a quick stop at our lockers that was one part dropping off books we didn't need and three parts lip gloss and hair check, we were on our way to a newspaper meeting.

I'd been on the school paper since I was old enough to form sentences. That's not an exaggeration; in first grade, I'd spearheaded my own handwritten newsletter that my father Xeroxed so I could distribute copies to my classmates. Now that we were less than a week out from the jubilee Naming Day, you could bet I wasn't going to miss the meeting where the entire staff of the

Masthead divvied up coverage of what was definitely going to be one of the biggest events of the year.

"I just miss her when she's buried in work, that's all. She puts so much into it."

Daisy elbowed me lightly. "That's something you two have in common, huh?"

"Yeah, yeah." I could be pretty strong-willed when it came to things I cared about—journalism school, seemingly unsolvable mysteries—and Daisy and Lena rarely passed up an opportunity to point it out.

She flashed me a grin that I caught in my peripheral vision. "You have to loosen up, girl," she said. "Plus, I have some *real* family drama for you."

"Ooh, do tell."

"You want *real* weird?"

"Always." We'd reached the third-floor landing and I jumped in front of her to pull the door open, looking at her curiously as she stepped through.

"Let's just say my parents were unthrilled to hear I'd been cast in the reenactment." She tried to play it off as no big deal, but I knew how excited Daisy was about the show, and I could read the disappointment on her face.

"That's crazy," I protested. I paused. "It *is* crazy, right? I know they can be . . . protective sometimes." It wasn't a secret that Daisy's family was strange. But it also wasn't something the rest of us went out of our way to highlight. "They knew you were trying out, right?"

She shrugged. "They had to. I brought it up a few times at home. Not to mention"—she looked at me, uncomfortable—"there's the whole 'Dewitt' thing in the first place."

I put a hand on her shoulder. "It's okay, Daisy," I said, smiling. "I know your family's important to this town. I agree—it would be bizarre if they hadn't expected you to be cast." A darker thought crossed my mind. "Wait—they didn't tell you not to do it, did they?" But no, of course not. A crisis of that magnitude would have been the first thing Daisy mentioned when I saw her. When they'd forbidden her from participating in our holiday choir back in fifth grade, Daisy had wept for hours on Lena's canopy bed.

As expected, she shook her head. "Definitely not—I think they knew it would be pointless, anyway, given how excited I was. But they were *not* into hearing about it. Mom, in particular, turned a terrifying shade of green when I tried to tell her about the script."

"Yikes."

"Serious yikes. I don't get it—especially given that the event is basically an ode to our ancestors, right?" She wrinkled her brow. "Maybe they just think it's, like . . . unseemly or something."

"That could be it." A family of eccentric homebodies might not be into a town play celebrating the awesomeness of their very own history. Then again, we celebrated Naming Day every year. What would their objection be to *this* year's reenactment? Was it just that Daisy was poised to star in it?

The slight sag in Daisy's shoulders told me that her parents' lack of enthusiasm was bothering her more than she wanted to let on. I tossed an arm over her shoulder, hoping to be reassuring. "Maybe *you* were just overreacting, like me. Something in the air this weekend. I bet when they see you up onstage, they'll be super into it."

"Maybe." Daisy sighed. I could smell the rosy notes of her shampoo. "From your lips to—"

A crackling sound, ominous and sharp like a rumble of thunder, from overhead cut Daisy off. It was followed by a *pop*, short and staccato, and a shriek from Daisy. On instinct I jumped back, pulling Daisy with me.

"What the . . ." My gaze darted around the space as I tried to figure out what was going on.

There was another *pop*, and a shattering sound, and then small shards of . . . *something* were hailing down on us. The smell of smoke, acrid and dense, filled the air.

"Watch out!" Daisy called. "It's the light." She backed against the wall, ramrod straight against the cold cinder blocks, and pointed.

Overhead, I saw what she was indicating: It was a light, just like she'd said—one of the large, rectangular fluorescent fixtures. Blackened, smoke-scorched, but otherwise . . . alarmingly indistinct.

"I guess it . . . blew out," she said after we'd both calmed down a little bit. My heart was no longer threatening to explode out of my chest, but the two of us were still breathing like we'd just finished a marathon.

"Yeah," I said slowly. "Except . . . I've never seen a light blow out as . . . *dramatically* as that one. Like, with extreme prejudice."

Almost as though it had been . . . I don't know, *waiting* to shatter at the very second Daisy and I happened to pass beneath it.

It *hadn't* been, of course—that was totally illogical.

But even with that being true, my heart was still leapfrogging at the back of my throat.

I was trying to joke, hoping that my voice didn't betray how unsettled the explosion had left me feeling. Lightbulbs blew out, yes—that was just a fact of living in this modern world of ours. But this one hadn't blown out so much as it had *exploded* directly overhead, to the point that Daisy and I were currently both aggressively brushing shards of glass out of our hair and off of our shoulders.

I glanced around: no exposed wires, no flickering lights other than the one that had just freaked out, no smoke that I could see, except from the burned-out fixture.

"Ouch!" Daisy said, holding up one finger for examination. "I cut myself." The cut was tiny, but blood quickly pooled and spilled down her finger. "It's fine. It's small. Just a drop. But—how crazy!" She looked at me. "You *cannot* mention this in front of my parents."

"Extremely crazy," I said. "And I won't." I was still trying to will my pulse back down to a reasonable rate. The drop of blood on her finger felt ominous, like a fairy-tale omen.

She gave her hair one final, cautious shake. "We should probably let, like, the office know, so they can send maintenance to come clean up." She shook her head, considering. "It's amazing we weren't hurt."

I glanced up again, where the fixture was *still* smoking, curls of black snaking out from the blown bulb. "It is," I agreed. "Come on. We can call from the *Masthead* meeting." Keene High School was almost as old as the town itself, and even in the age of iPhones, the inter-class telephones were still fully functional and used on the regular.

I filed away the details of the scene and put them in a tiny lockbox in the back of my brain. In the absence of any actual clues to solve, there was nothing to do but forge ahead.

Daisy delicately sidestepped the various piles of glass as she gave me a knowing smirk. "Typical Nancy Drew," she said. "Never let anything get in the way of a scoop."

"You say that like it's a bad thing."

CHAPTER FOUR

By the time the *Masthead* meeting was in full swing, I'd regained my composure. Or, at least, well enough to fake it. After digging a Band-Aid out of my bag for Daisy, I had called down to the office, and the secretary promised the light would be cleaned up right away. It was hard to convey to her how spectacular the whole incident has been, so that was the best we could expect. All of which meant that Daisy and I both were fully free to jump into *Masthead* mode, unfettered. We'd agreed not to bog the meeting down with any discussion of what happened in the hall. These meetings dragged on forever as it was.

Jumping right in, I perched at my normal spot, on top of the teacher's desk at the front of the room scribbling notes on my spiral reporter's pad, stopping intermittently to point at people as I referenced them in my diatribe. "So, that's me on reenactment coverage," I said, reviewing, "Melanie on the founding families' profiles, Theo on—"

"Seriously, Drew, I'm fine sitting this one out." Theo MacCabe, our resident disaffected emo boy, flashed me a pleading look.

Theo, Seth Farrell, and Melanie Forest rounded out the editorial board alongside Daisy, Lena, and me. Being a self-proclaimed contrarian, Theo was almost always guaranteed to run counter to popular opinion, so that made him vital to our staff. I'm all about journalistic objectivity, which means *fair and balanced* representation. But sometimes, his rage-against-the-machine stance was exhausting.

Like now. I sighed. "Are you *sure*?" I shouldn't have been surprised. The shattered light had knocked me off my game, clearly.

I wasn't the only one unimpressed by Theo's antagonistic tendencies. The entire staff of the *Masthead* was shooting Theo variations on the expression I assumed was plastered across my own face too.

"You're, like . . . the Grinch of Naming Day." Daisy looked like she was taking his disdain personally.

"You're too kind, Daisy," Lena put in. "Everyone knows the Grinch eventually comes around."

"Well, then I guess that makes you Cindy Lou Who," Theo said. He ran a hand through his dark hair, letting it flop over one eye in a move that seemed calculatedly casual to me. I stifled an eye roll as he narrowed his gaze at Daisy. "I know who I'd rather be in that scenario."

Melanie, another self-proclaimed theater geek who Daisy was friendly with after so many years of costarring in school productions, chimed in, rolling her eyes. "We get it, Theo, you're above the whole Naming Day thing, and you'd rather spend that weekend brooding around Hot Topic and listening to sad eighties whine-rock. That just means one less person to compete with over pieces, so go with God, if you ask me." A few others echoed their agreement with this sentiment.

Theo straightened in his seat, bristling. "I *am* above it," he said. "And you should be too." He literally pointed an accusing finger, like a villager in the third act of an outdated Disney movie. "It's such a sad, sycophantic display of misplaced ethnocentrism, thinly disguised as town pride." It was impressive, the way he spat it out, multisyllabic phrasing and all.

"Points for the twenty-dollar word, brother," a voice broke into the din. "But you have to know you're not winning any popularity points with this tactic."

I swiveled as everyone else in the room also turned, nearly in unison, to see who'd made that comment.

Well, hello.

Parker Winslow was a transfer student, new this year, and though we didn't have any classes together, I knew all about him—originally from Chicago, had gone national in fencing, which was unusual but inarguably cool, had a much older sister who worked for a nonprofit in Miami. Horseshoe Bay is a small town, and newcomers are rare. And newcomers who bear a striking resemblance to a lesser-known Hemsworth brother?

Yeah, you're going to hear about them. Especially if you're me, and digging is your thing.

Seeing, though? Up close and personal? That was different from hearing. *Way* different.

Rumors had *definitely* not been exaggerated. Now that he was standing in the *Masthead* doorway, I realized I'd never been this close to him before. His eyes were a color I'd never seen before on a human face, some green/blue/gray mix that seemed to change with every micromovement he made. His hair was a sandy blondish brown, perfectly tousled. I found myself idly wondering what it would feel like to run my fingers through it. . . .

Get it together, Drew.

This was weird. I mean, I'd had boyfriends before, though nothing all that serious. And it wasn't like I'd never been in the same room with a cute guy before. But this felt . . . next level, somehow. Like the air pressure had dropped since he'd walked in. There went all that composure I was so happily pretending to have recaptured.

Not good. I had a *Masthead* issue to put out and a Naming Day to help plan, and exactly no time for hair tousling, fantasized or otherwise.

Lena, however, seemed to be immune to his whole pressure-y aura. She looked at him, scanning dispassionately. "While I know we all appreciate the vote of solidarity," she said, "I don't know that we need a peanut gallery swinging by just to weigh in."

Parker smiled. The backs of my knees tingled, a spot on my body I previously hadn't known *could* tingle.

This is the opposite of getting it together.

"I can see how it might seem that way to you," he said, still giving that light, easy grin, "but I'm here to join the team."

"And we love . . . joiners," I said, wincing. "But the thing is, Naming Day coverage has all been assigned." Cute or no, I was defensive of my bylines.

"Well, yeah," he said. "I heard some of that, as I was—well, lurking," he finished, sheepish.

Oh, he gave such good "sheepish."

"But then I heard your boy Theo, here, insisting that he didn't want the beat, so I'm going to assume you have a hole in your schedule." He looked at me. "Didn't want you to be left high and dry."

"Real talk: It wouldn't be hard to fill," Lena said, dangling it like a threat—one that we all knew was empty.

"He wants the beat," I put in, still in some kind of weird, unnecessary denial.

"'He' *doesn't*," Theo replied, insistent. He stood now, bouncing on his heels, warming to his little riff. "'He' keeps saying it too. I genuinely am not interested in covering Naming Day or anything to do with it."

"I . . . don't understand," Daisy said blankly.

Theo gave a short laugh, his shoulders shaking. "I'm sure you don't." He looked at her. "Do you have to take some kind of, like, blood oath of Horseshoe Bay fealty, as a Dewitt? Because I'm picturing it a lot like a baptism but with sixty percent more creepy religious overtones."

Ouch. Don't hold back, Theo.

I glanced at Daisy. Her lower lip was trembling, though she

was trying to play it off. If we as a town took homegrown pride seriously, then Daisy's family lived the extended-play dance remix of that base-level pride. And the "creepy religious over-tones"? That was a little too close to home.

"Are the rest of us supposed to apologize for *not* coming from tragic broken homes?" Lena put in, coming to Daisy's defense before I had the chance to. "Just because *you* need to be all rebel-without-a-cause twenty-four seven doesn't mean Naming Day isn't a big deal to a lot of us."

"Oh, but see—that's where you're wrong," Theo countered. "I'm downright lousy with causes."

"'Lousy' being the key word, there," I said. Whether or not our town had a unique tendency to overhype the Naming Day phenomenon, Daisy was right—the last thing we needed was a Grinch in our midst. That sort of negativity was infectious.

"Maybe it's a little silly how into town history everyone here is," I said, "but who cares? It's tradition. And it's *fun*. You know . . . *fun*? Like: a good time? You should try it."

Parker stepped forward, giving me a smooth smile that made my cheeks feel flushed. "Don't overexert yourself, Nancy. You can lead a buzzkill to the celebration, but you can't take the stick out of his—"

I stifled a laugh, clinging to a last grasp at professionalism.

What is happening to you?

"Look, dude," Theo said, "I don't know who you even are, but you're not even *on* the *Masthead* staff. So maybe back off with your witty critiques of me or the way I approach my beat."

"Actually," Parker said, shooting me a tentative look, "as of today, I officially *am* on the *Masthead*'s . . . er, masthead."

"It's a double entendre," I said. "Nautical term."

"Believe it or not, while we may not all be savants on par with the local girl sleuth, that much I knew," Parker replied. Though he was definitely teasing, flames crawled up my cheeks. Yes, I had a reputation around Horseshoe Bay. But no, I didn't love when cute new boys got wind of that rep before they'd had a chance to get to know me. *Perfect.*

Theo looked nonplussed. "I'm sorry, so you're on the ed board?" He looked at me, throwing up his hands. "When did *that* happen?"

"Not the ed board, the writing staff," Parker said. "It happened when I asked Mr. Pitilli to sponsor my application."

Theo looked at me. "Nancy!"

I shrugged. "What do you want me to do? If Pitilli signed his application form, he's in. You know as well as I do, it's policy."

It was. The buck started and stopped with me, as EIC, when it came to assigning articles. But anyone who wanted to could apply to our writing pool, as long as they had a teacher's sponsorship. Pitilli taught AP Lit and, frankly, was notoriously a little bit of a hard-ass. If *he* was Parker's sponsor, I felt good about Parker joining the team.

"Great," Theo said sarcastically. "Another lemming, then?"

Parker just shrugged. "If by 'lemming,' you mean: 'Keene High student who's stoked about Naming Day and happy to cover it'? Then yeah."

"*Thank* you," Daisy said, relieved. "At least someone here has a sense of occasion."

"*Someone?*" Theo scoffed. "More like the whole damn town. And it's a total waste of energy—not to mention ink—if you ask me—"

"Literally no one asked you," Lena pointed out.

Melanie stood up, holding an extended arm out like she was directing traffic. "Okay, listen, he's entitled to his opinion," she said. "There's no reason to get hostile." She and Theo were tight—their families were old friends—even if they didn't see eye to eye on this particular issue.

Daisy shook her head. "He's the hostile one. I mean, hate on tradition all you want, but this is still an important issue for us. If you're gonna be such a downer, why even come to the meeting?"

Theo raised his eyebrows. "So these things are optional? I hadn't realized."

"They're not," I confirmed quickly. "But there's, you know, lively debate and dissent, and then there's pot-stirring just for the sake of causing drama."

"Right. I always forget how expressing a different view from the popular opinion is just 'causing drama.'"

"Oh my *God*, can you please just get over yourself for a *minute?*" Lena said, her voice rising in frustration.

"Guys," I cut in, "this is super not-helpful—"

"Well, sure, if our resident Holden Caulfield is just going to hunch in the corner throwing shade . . . ," Lena said, eyes flashing.

My gazed whipped back and forth as I considered how best to break this up. With every second that passed, that seemed like more and more of an impossibility. Just as I was about to fully *stand* up on the teacher's desk and give some kind of elaborate whistle, the room was rocked by a startling *thud* at the window. We all flinched and turned.

"What was *that*?" Daisy asked, her voice small. She was still on edge from the explosion in the hallway, but it would have been startling either way.

We all exchanged tentative glances. A crash that loud had only a few obvious causes. A bird, chances were. Flying straight into the glass. Another unpleasant metaphor. But it had been so *loud*. Like, improbably so.

We stood stock-still, no one wanting to be the first to peer out the window and investigate-slash-confirm.

Well, no one except me.

"Okay," Parker said, breaking the loaded silence. "If nothing else, it was the end of *that* argument, right?"

Right.

It wasn't much of a silver lining. But we didn't have anything else.

CHAPTER FIVE

We'd had a cat when I was little—a fat striped tabby I named Sprinkles—who'd liked to leave me little gifts of half-eaten prey: sparrow heads and chipmunks with their rib cages stripped raw splayed out at the front door, flecks of blood still clinging to the tips of her whiskers. This couldn't be any worse than *that*.

Right?

I took a deep breath. "It was a bird," I said, crossing to the far side of the room to open the window and peer out. "I'm sure of—"

I swallowed.

For a moment, I couldn't find the rest of that sentence. *I'm sure of it.* Because looking out the window had confirmed what I was sure of with horrifying, gruesome clarity.

"*Is* it a bird? Nancy?" Daisy's voice trembled, uncertain. "It is, right? It left a crack in the window."

I glanced up to where she was pointing and blinked, not quite believing what I was seeing. Because there *was* a crack in the window, a sizable chunk, spreading into an ominous web that twisted and branched from the initial point of impact.

"*Is* it a bird?" Lena echoed, tiptoeing up behind me. "Because I've *never* seen a bird damage a window like that. What was it, a hawk?"

She was joking. But she wasn't that far off, improbable as it seemed.

"Close," I said grimly.

I pushed the window as far up as it would go and swung my legs over until I was outside, feet touching down on the overgrown grass. I kneeled down to have a better look and immediately flashed back to one of Sprinkles's most violent kills: a rabbit, gray and small, one eye gouged out, the gory socket crawling with bugs.

This was slightly less bloody than the rabbit had been. That was something, at least.

Sometimes it's the little things.

"What is it?" It was Parker, his voice way steadier than either of my friends' had been. He was at the window, craning to have a better look.

My gaze caught on something—minuscule, easy to overlook, but then again, I was nothing if not observant. I swiftly plucked the something in question from the bird and examined it, careful not to touch the carcass in the process. I stood to find everyone lined up at the window, expectant and nervous, a row of anxious shoulders and worried expressions.

"I think it's a raven," I told them. A hawk's shadier, goth-styled cousin. And not particularly common around here.

"What?" Parker hopped out the window to have a look of his own. "Holy crap."

I know. My formal knowledge of ornithology was sorely lacking, but I could say with some real certainty that I didn't know the last time I'd encountered a raven outside of an Edgar Allan Poe poem or the Halloween decorations section of the party store.

We stared in silence together, for a moment. As grotesque as the scene was, it was hard to look away.

It *was* a raven, sure enough: huge, ink-black feathers looking oil-slick in the afternoon sun. And it *had* hit the window with enough force to shatter it, and in the process, it had . . . well, it had nearly taken its entire head off too. In fact, its head had twisted so far around that now it clung by little more than a few bloody threads, one glassy eye gazing blankly into space.

The bird also was—or it had been, before the . . . decapitation—wearing a collar. Something skinny and leather-looking. Brown. Which was *still* not the strangest thing about the whole situation.

Parker looked at me. "What was that thing, though?"

I looked at him. "What do you mean?"

"You—you pulled something. From the bird."

"I . . ." I trailed off. I couldn't remember the last time someone had *caught* me doing something that was meant to be under the radar. Parker spotting me grab the note was almost like him walking in on me changing in the gym locker room—I felt that exposed.

"It's . . ." I paused, totally unsettled. *This* was the strangest part, so bizarre I really wasn't sure how to proceed—and that was before being stripped down (metaphorically speaking) by this mysterious new hottie. "Um. Well, it's a note." I nodded in response to everyone's confused faces. "Yeah. There was a note in its beak."

"*Oookay.* So, what does it say?" Daisy called, straining her torso as far out the window as she could.

Reluctantly, I unfolded the square of paper again. A few stray drops of blood stained one corner, and I gingerly did my best to avoid them.

"'Beware the Naming Day curse,'" I read, voice as flat as I could make it. If I could stay calm, maybe this would all seem twenty percent less creepy?

It's a theory, anyway.

I didn't want to read the rest of the note, like saying the words out loud would give them a power I wasn't prepared for. And I knew the reaction I'd get from everyone gathered around.

But not reading the note wouldn't cause it to cease to exist. It was real, in my hands, and it couldn't have come to us by accident.

I coughed, cleared my throat. *"Naming Day must be called off."*

"So, this is a joke, right?" Half an hour—and a *ton* of debate—later, Daisy was somehow still holding out hope.

We were still inside the *Masthead* classroom (those of us who'd gone out the window safely back inside by now), this time with desks pulled into a circle that felt protective and necessary. I'd locked the classroom door too. The note—creepy, bloodstained, hand-scrawled in shaky lettering—sat on my desk in front of me, those words blaring at me accusingly.

"It's got to be a joke," Lena repeated, though she was still up-talking like she was asking a question, and she didn't sound very confident. "The Naming Day curse? What even is that?"

I'd been asking myself that very same question since we'd opened the note that the raven had carried. Horseshoe Bay was *my* town; I knew it better than the back of my hand. I knew its every legend, every tall tale, every ghost story.

Or so I'd thought.

The idea that there was a curse I'd never even *heard* of? That was maybe more worrying than the idea of a curse itself. A curse, I can disprove. A surprise?

Well . . . a surprise was harder to get over.

"How do you jokingly send a creepy, note-carrying *raven* into a classroom window?" Melanie said, her voice squeaking. "Like, who even knows how to do that? That is some Southern Gothic horror novel nonsense." I knew she was literally a drama queen, but her response to the bird had been heightened; she was sitting up straighter, her voice just a few octaves higher than everyone else's, since the bird had appeared.

An excellent question. Also on my mind: Was there a reason this whole incident was piquing something in some far-flung corner of my frontal lobe? Déjà vu or something similar gnawed at me like an itch between my shoulder blades that I just couldn't reach. But *what?* Ravens weren't a bird I thought much about once I'd passed eighth-grade English.

"It *is* very *Game of Thrones*," Parker said. Of everyone in the room, he seemed the least taken aback by the maybe-harbinger bird's appearance. I tried not to think about what that could mean.

He should be shocked. My brain's autoplay was stuck on that thought. He should be shocked, because it was legitimately shocking—even to me, and I've seen things—and everyone else was straight-up horrified. Putting aside the fact that a mutilated raven at the window was the stuff of a medieval dream sequence . . . the fact that it had, apparently, been carrying a warning, Greek-tragedy-style?

It was concerning.

One might even say it had the makings of the first stirrings of a mystery.

But I didn't want to say that, not out loud. Not just yet.

Not everyone would see it as good news, the way I did. Not everyone enjoyed mysteries. And Daisy would be crushed at the idea of anything interfering with her Naming Day, her year.

"It's an . . . odd choice for a joke," Seth said. "In that it's not funny. And how did that bird get to *us*, anyway?"

"Maybe it wasn't for us," Daisy said. She was jittery, but then, so were we all.

"It was carrying a *note*," Melanie pointed out. "*Someone* sent it out into the great wide yonder with deliberateness. Straight to the window of the *Masthead* office. If it wasn't for us, then who?"

Daisy attempted a shrug, but I knew her well enough to see that she was trying a bit too hard to be casual. "If it were a prank, like Lena said, it wouldn't have mattered what window it hit or who found it, right? It would just be meant to, like, mess with kids at Keene High, get them all worked up in the lead-up to Naming Day."

I looked at Lena. "You *really* think that's all it was?"

She frowned, considering. "I feel like . . . I mean, even just the fact that it mentions some random 'curse' . . . ," Lena said. "That's not even a thing. Hence: prank."

"Maybe," I hedged. "But if so, it's a pretty *elaborate* prank, don't you think? A carrier bird? A *raven*? You don't see many of those around here, generally speaking."

Except . . . Except for that nagging itch, still buzzing just below the surface, telling me that there was maybe something, some small detail here that I was missing.

I can't lie: the prospect? It was unnerving, yes. But it was also *thrilling*.

A missed hint is basically the prologue of a mystery. Which meant that even if it *was* just a prank? I was *for sure* going to investigate.

"You're saying you can't think of anyone who'd put that much effort into a prank?" Melanie asked. "Have you forgotten last homecoming, when the football team managed to *suspend the principal's car from one of the goalposts* on the football field?"

"Okay," I agreed. "But that was hilarious high school hijinks. This is . . . disgusting, and obviously meant to freak people out. Possibly *us* specifically. So not only would the prankster need to be *totally* motivated to pull something like this off, he or she would *also* need to be hard-core anti–Naming Day in order to even *want* to upset us—or whomever the prank was specifically intended for, in the first place—so badly." I look around. "Can any of us think of someone who might be cynical enough to do something like that?"

One by one, we all turned toward Theo. As he realized we were all staring at him, an angry flush crept up his neck. "God, *no!*" he protested. "I mean, yeah, I think Naming Day is lame, but I *promise* you, this is not my style." He smiled wryly. "Honestly, I'm flattered you'd even think of me for this one, but I swear, I'm way too lazy to put in this kind of effort. For anything."

"Fair," I said. "Your words, not mine." He didn't flinch from my gaze; he was definitely being sincere. I considered what I knew of him. Theo's op-ed pieces were on point, but he never, ever went a single syllable over his target word count. He wasn't exactly industrious. So he was probably telling the truth now. *But if not Theo, then who?*

Just off the top of my head, I could only think of one other person who'd seemed as put out by Naming Day—or at least, by certain aspects of it—as Theo had.

"Caroline Mark," I said, considering. "She completely flipped out yesterday on the quad when she didn't get cast in the reenactment. Like in a *big* way. You guys saw." I looked at

Daisy and Lena, who both nodded. "What are the chances *she* has access to a fleet of birds?"

"It was *definitely* her," Daisy said, jumping up. "It had to be. It's like you say: She was furious, and this prank needed fury. Who else could it have been?"

Good question. I wasn't sure I was so ready to close the book on our suspect list just yet, but Daisy was right—there were no other obvious suspects.

"She did have motive," I said. "Jealousy's one of the classics, after all." It was means and opportunity I was wondering about, but Daisy was off on a tear by now.

"Exactly!" Daisy said enthusiastically. "It must be her! In which case, we have nothing to worry about."

"Bird flu notwithstanding," Parker quipped.

Daisy waved at him dismissively. "I realize you're joking," she said, "but trust me, Nancy didn't touch that bird when she picked up the note. Our girl is way too careful for that."

I shrugged. "It's true." I'm all too well trained in navigating a prospective crime scene.

"And obviously, Caroline Mark is just a sad, disgruntled wannabe who needed to get a little bit of sad—and gross— revenge before she could get over getting left off the reenact-ment cast list."

"A sad, disgruntled wannabe who's sending birds to their death in order to pass along creepy, threatening messages," Seth pointed out. "I think we have to do something. We can't just ignore this."

"Do something like what?" Melanie asked. "Confront her? Tell the principal?"

He shrugged. "Or something. Right?" He looked at me. "I can't be the only one who thinks that."

I took a breath, considering how to respond. In my experience, I tended to have better luck investigating these things on my own than including the so-called authorities. But that note . . . even if it *was* a joke, it was sick. Disturbing.

"Just—not yet!" Daisy blurted. At Seth's incredulous look, she went on, imploring. "I—I hear what you're saying, and yeah, it's weird, and okay, maybe we do have to tell someone. *Eventually.*"

"Dais—" I started, but she cut me off.

"*Eventually*," she repeated. "But do we have to do it right now? Hear me out," she said, seeing Seth open his mouth to reply. "If we say something to the principal, the reenactment *might* actually be canceled. You never know. It's a small town. There are some majorly superstitious people living here. And even though *some* people"—she shot a dirty look at Theo—"think it's just a stupid little folk tradition, I've literally been looking forward to my own reenactment forever." She lowered her voice. "Please, let's not mess up my chance to perform?"

Now she looked at me specifically, her eyes wide. "*Please*, let's not do anything to ruin the festival. For me?"

For me. My stomach sank; it was the one thing she could say that would pretty much always get me to stop dead in my tracks. I knew Daisy better than I knew myself sometimes. She wasn't exaggerating when she said she'd been waiting her whole damn life to be in the reenactment.

"Maybe . . . we could put a pin in telling anyone," I offered finally. "*For now.* Wait and see." I made my tone stern. "If *anything* else happens, though—"

Daisy cut me off. "If *anything* else happens, totally," she gushed, relief pouring from her in palpable waves.

"If anything else happens, I have to admit, I'll be curious to see it," Theo said. "When you start with a dead bird, you've set the bar pretty high."

"Agreed," Parker said. He flashed a quick, unreadable glance my way. Was he sympathetic? Curious? Did he think I was wrong to agree to brush this incident aside? I couldn't tell.

And I couldn't remember the last time I'd cared about some guy's opinion this much either.

Joke's on him, though. And Daisy, too.

Because the thing was: All I had agreed to was not saying anything about the raven to anyone else just yet. An easy concession to make, all told. I hadn't agreed with Daisy that our culprit was definitely Caroline Mark. And I *definitely* hadn't said anything about writing off this newly minted town curse as harmless, meaningless local lore. Personally, while I didn't believe in anything not grounded in fact, I absolutely believed that almost all urban legends *were* grounded in truth.

Clearly, someone out there agreed with me. At least enough to stick that note on the bird, prank or no. Which meant that I had my work cut out for me.

First things first.

Dig into the details of this so-called Naming Day curse. There's a story there.

And where there's a story?

A mystery often follows.

CHAPTER SIX

wake to the sound of rain: driving, insistent, heavy.
I've left the windows open, and moist air dances around me as
the curtains gyrate in the wind. The house is still—so still, I'm
instantly sure I'm the only one awake.

It's not *my* bedroom, I realize, but it feels familiar, even
though I couldn't say how or why. The floors are wood, wide-
planked and sturdy-looking, and beyond the windows, I hear a
persistent banging.

I turn to flip the nightstand lamp on—small, glass-based,
with a frilly lampshade more old-fashioned than anything my
parents would have in our house. The room takes on a low glow.
I tiptoe toward the window. . . . There's an urgent sound, a rustling on the wind, and shadows play across the darkened walls.

Birds?

It shouldn't be the first place my mind goes to (should it?), but now that it *has*, that rustling . . . It's undeniable . . . It's the sound of—

I step back, crouch down. Brace myself.

Birds. A flock of them. More. Black wings beating, the flapping causing that rhythmic patter in the background. They swoop through the open window, into the room, at me.

It's a scene straight from a Hitchcock classic—dark, frantic wings thudding at my skin with startling force. Beaks darting and dipping, pecking at my flesh, leaving me pockmarked and bleeding. I open my mouth to scream, but the birds—their greasy feathers, the grit of the dirt that clings to their talons—they're on my tongue, choking me, forcing me to swallow back silent shrieks and unshed tears.

The rhythm of the birds swooping through the window becomes increasingly frantic, and I hear their bodies pound at the walls, pushing and wriggling their way in like an impossible tidal wave. They fill the room like water, chirping and screeching hideously, making my skin crawl. Soon they cover every inch of the bedroom, and I've curled myself into a ball at the foot of the bed, my knees drawn to my chin and my arms cradling my head, ignoring the vicious pecking and the warm, wet sensation of blood oozing down my arms. I can't scream; that much is clear. I don't dare move a muscle. I'm trapped.

The floorboards groan under the weight of us all—the birds, me, the heat and the violence contained in this oh-so-finite space—and the floor beneath me buckles, and for a moment I truly fear it's going to give way, sending me plummeting to whatever lies below.

And though the thought is chilling, it's also something I might welcome, if it were to offer even a minute of relief from these birds—

"At ease!" I hear, a strong, steady voice. Confident. It calls to the birds, commands them, and incredibly, impossibly, they respond. Like the snap of my fingers, or the flip of a switch, they're gone, and I'm alone in the room again, battered, gasping for air, trying to comprehend what's just happened. I hear a rattling sound, tin, and I open my mouth again. *What's that?* I want to ask, but I can still taste the feathers in the back of my throat, and the words seem to be stuck. I cough, prepare to try again, and—

I sat up in bed, panting and soaked with sweat.

What the hell?

A dream, obviously—or, more to the point, a nightmare. Which, for the record, I never have. But I guess there's a first time for everything.

Leave it to *my* subconscious to be borderline lazy with its subtext. *Dreaming about killer birds the same day a bird commits kamikaze outside of your classroom? Do tell me more, Dr. Freud.*

It was a gross dream, yeah. But it was not a subtle one. And *only* a dream, at that. Still, though—I took a moment to sneak a glance at my bedroom window (*my* bedroom now, for real, yet another sign that back in the here and now there was literally nothing to be afraid of) and was almost embarrassed at how relieved I felt to see that the window was closed *and* locked.

Just a dream. Even if that weird feeling of déjà vu from the newspaper meeting was still lingering like seafoam after the crash of a wave.

I shuddered. I could still taste the oily feathers.

Sometimes having a vivid imagination is a blessing. Like when you're solving a mystery. Examine every angle, consider every clue . . . Other times, it's a serious burden. Like when you wake to the lingering effects of a nasty nightmare.

I took a deep breath.

The nightmare was gross, but it wasn't *really* what was gnawing at me. My subconscious may have been ironically skating along at surface level, but I knew, in my gut, what was truly eating away at the back of my mind.

The Naming Day curse.

Daisy might not have wanted to dig deeper into this thing, but I wasn't Daisy. Sitting on the sidelines has never been my thing.

The key to getting to the bottom of the raven? Getting to the bottom of the curse itself. And sure, it was, like—I glanced at the clock on my nightstand—1:47 a.m. But as the saying goes, *no time like the present.*

I padded into my dad's study, taking care to avoid the squeaky floorboard just outside my parents' bedroom on my way. He wasn't wild about people getting into his personal space, but what he didn't know couldn't hurt him. Normally, I'd just use my own trusty laptop, but it had done some weird freeze-y thing the other day and was still in the shop. Not ideal timing for an active investigation. I just had to hope no one woke up and asked me what I was up to.

One thing working in my favor: I knew my dad's passwords— he rotated between variations on his and Mom's anniversary and my birthday, which any security expert would no doubt say was a truly terrible idea. But he seemed to think everyone in his life was totally and completely trustworthy. It was cute, really.

Did that knowledge give me a twinge of guilt in my side as I tapped at the keyboard and watched as the password prompt gave way to an enormous wallpaper of the three of us, beaming away, the candles of my sixteenth birthday cake casting a glow over our smiling faces?

Sure. But just a twinge.

Horseshoe Bay curse. I typed the phrase into the search engine and hit return.

Immediately, three pages of hits appeared.

Jackpot.

Or, er—jackpot-adjacent? I frowned, scanning the headlines, which were all, maddeningly, about Dead Lucy. Okay, sure, she was famous—or maybe "notorious" was the better word. But she was just one dead girl.

Not to be callous. But one dead girl does not a curse make. A lurid headline or seven? Sure. A deliciously morbid urban legend? Absolutely. But a curse? Not so much.

And yet—a seemingly endless scroll of Dead Lucy headlines passed beneath the cursor as I moved the mouse.

It wasn't until the last page of search results that I found it. One single, solitary hit that just happened to be about the Naming Day curse. An opinion piece in an old, now-defunct newspaper from Horseshoe Bay's days of yore, the *Horseshoe Bay Tribune*. It had gone bankrupt when I was still in grade school, which seemed to be the way the tide was turning with print journalism. Not that that fact made me any less eager to study it once I went off to college. On the contrary—the idea that truth in journalism was faltering along with the media industry itself made me want to pursue it all the more. Call me a glutton for punishment.

One hit—but just the one. Any other reasonable, well-adjusted human being might have found that disturbing—or at least a mild bummer.

Me? I couldn't resist a quick fist pump before I clicked the link. One hit is better than no hits, when you're desperately searching for leads.

Loading . . . loading . . . My father was one of the most renowned lawyers in Horseshoe Bay, but he was also a low-key Luddite. My mother claimed she found it charming. But she was generally nicer than I was. I could admit it.

And then it was there, flashing. ERROR: 404. PAGE NOT FOUND. With a giant, blaring red X and a frowny face.

Interesting.

The "girl sleuth" side of me couldn't help but see this latest roadblock as a challenge to be conquered, even as the "regular, curious person" in me was frustrated beyond belief.

This was the twenty-first century, after all. Putting aside my dad's own weird, intermittent mistrust of so-called newfangled technology, *how* did an urban legend—no matter how obscure—manage to avoid an online footprint?

Very, very interesting.

Frustration was quickly being overridden by that little shiver I get at the back of my neck just at the moment that I realize I'm on the trail of a new case.

So the Naming Day curse was a no go, at least as far as the Internet was concerned.

Okay.

I'd solved plenty of puzzles with way less to go on.

I closed out the browser tab, taking care to clear my search history. My father was alarmingly trustworthy, sure, but a good detective always covers her tracks.

The lack of information about the Naming Day curse was downright bizarre. And "downright bizarre" was my *jam*. I was going to do a deep dive, learn everything and anything there was to know about this curse. First thing tomorrow.

Maybe I should have been worried. Maybe I should have been scared. After all, at least one person had already tried to spook me (and the rest of my team on the newspaper) off the trail of this story.

But I don't scare easily. Instead, I investigate.

And that's just what I was going to do.

CHAPTER SEVEN

Tuesday

'm sorry, dear," Ms. Beekman, our school librarian, was saying, sounding anything but. "It's just that I can't very well give you something I don't actually have, myself. Surely you must understand that."

"Surely," I grumbled, hating to admit as much aloud. I took a deep breath, willing myself to be patient with her. If our school had been founded at the turn of the last century, Ms. Beekman would have been around and behind the reference desk at least since then. Or so the story went. She was sweet, but there was a scent of decay to her aura that was barely masked by the peppermint hard candies she kept in her desk drawer.

I adjusted my messenger bag against my hip, determined to at least give it another try. "It's just—the *Tribune*. It was small, okay. Not winning any Pulitzers. But it was a legitimate Horseshoe Bay publication, and this town is not without its steadfast demonstrations of pride. Case in point: Naming Day."

Ms. Beekman peered at me over those prim half-lens glasses women of her generation love to keep around their neck on a chain. "Well, sure, dear. But that's just the problem."

"Naming Day?" It was sure starting to seem like a problem for my friends and me.

She smiled. "No, sweetheart. That the paper—the *Tribune*— was a small periodical in an even smaller town. When it folded, so did any trace of its archives."

That's . . . unusual. Mind you, I was still a few years off from J-school, but the idea of a newspaper, no matter how small potatoes, simply ghosting into thin air couldn't have been *too* commonplace.

"What about microfiche?" I asked, growing a little more desperate than I cared to admit. Most research had been digitized by now, *thank God*, but a few of my cases—not to mention, a few book reports here and there—had led me to the back room of the Horseshoe Bay library, where the reels and reels of microfiche gathered dust.

"Oh, yes," Ms. Beekman said, nodding with surprising energy. "That would, of course, be the first place one would presumably think to look."

"Of course." I tried to match her energy. It was difficult and involved a lot of repression.

"But"—she sighed—"you'll recall there was that terrible fire in 2010. We were very fortunate; firefighters were able to extinguish it before it reached the second floor. But much of our back room—including several of the microfiche catalogues—was destroyed beyond repair. Even if the fire hadn't melted the materials, the smoke and water damage would have been . . . well." She shuddered and pulled her cardigan tighter over her shoulders, as though the mere thought of such a thing was way too traumatic to bear. "We're just lucky to have saved as much as we did."

"So lucky," I echoed, though the fact that they'd saved data that wasn't useful to me right now didn't exactly feel like a windfall for my purposes.

What now? "Can you think of any other place I might find old issues of the *Tribune*?" I asked—a hopeful Hail Mary.

"You might try online," she said, starting to sound more than a little bored with this conversation. "The Internet?"

"Yes, I've heard of it," I joked, softly enough that any barb in my tone went undetected. "I did look there," I said, realizing that I was working harder, now, not to sound testy. Was it my imagination, or was Beekman being a little . . . resistant? I knew I could sometimes get a little bit . . . uh, laser-focused when on a trail, so maybe I was projecting or reading into random, harmless things, but it was starting to feel like this librarian was playing at what my father might call a hostile witness.

Then again, maybe she was still holding a grudge from last spring, when I'd uncovered that mystery of the spurned cheerleader who'd hacked into the school's grading system and failed her cheating boyfriend out of calculus. The fact that the hacking had taken place in the school library apparently made Beekman look not-great, and it wouldn't have exactly been shocking to learn that she was not exactly a Nancy Drew fangirl.

"It was so strange," I went on, trying for a softer touch. "There was literally just the one hit. I mean, that never happens."

"I suppose it is rare," Ms. Beekman said, but her gaze was back to her desk, to her own keyboard, and she began tapping away, very obviously, over our conversation.

Her dwindling interest sparked something in me, made me want to rise to this weird, perceived challenged of maintaining her attention. "And then," I went on, loud enough that a few students sitting at a nearby table, studying, shot me a look, "when I clicked the link, it was broken."

"Hmm," she said noncommittally. "Well, you know what they say."

"Actually, Ms. Beekman, I'm not sure I do," I said, frustrated.

Now she looked up from her computer at last. Her blue eyes were watery, slightly bloodshot from age. "Curiosity killed the cat," she said.

Ouch.

Well, there was no mistaking *that* tone, at least. Whatever thinly veiled evasiveness she was practicing was no longer veiled. At all. And while that made this whole process that much harder . . .

It also made it more interesting. "Am *I* the cat in this scenario?" I asked.

She scooted her chair to one side so she could look more directly at me, which was more unnerving than I would have expected. "Darling, of course not," she said, her tone softer now. "It's only that . . . well, this is a small town. And like any small town, it has its traditions."

"Like Naming Day."

"Like Naming Day," she agreed. "And other . . . well, you know. The stories."

"Urban legends," I said. "Like Dead Lucy."

"Ghosts, yes. And other legends. The Naming Day curse is probably just another one of those. And, frankly, I guess I just don't see why you'd want to go poking around in all of that non-sense. Nothing good can come of it."

Well, she was wrong there. Poking around behind the scenes of just about anything or anywhere was pretty much my favor-ite. But it was slowly becoming clear to me: Beekman was hella superstitious. It made sense, and it wasn't uncommon among older neighbors of Horseshoe Bay. My grandmother had been the same way. Never crossing under a ladder, always throwing some spilled salt over one shoulder . . . silly little talismans meant to protect against the horrors and uncertainties of every-day life.

It didn't work, though. Salt over a shoulder didn't do much good when my grandfather's age caught up to him and his heart failed. Neither did prayer, though at the time I could tell that it gave my grandmother some comfort. And maybe that's what Beekman's superstitions were to her—comfort. An attempt to exert even the tiniest bit of control over a chaotic system.

The good news was that I could understand a little better

where she was coming from, especially thinking back to how my grandmother used to literally cross the street when she saw a black cat, or how she believed certain numbers were "lucky" and some were dangerous. In that context, Beekman's reluctance to help me dig in to this missing article made a little more sense.

The bad news was that just because I got it, didn't mean I was going to go along with it. I don't believe in superstitions, after all. Only facts.

I opened my mouth to push back, to ask, if nothing else, if she might have other ideas of places to check for backlogs of old town newspapers. City Hall was my first thought, but would they be more helpful—more forthcoming—than Beekman? I had to hope.

But I didn't have a chance to ask anything. Because before I could get a word out, I heard a scream.

I know that scream.

It was all I could think as I ran through the hallways, my bag banging against one leg as insistently as my heart hammered against my rib cage. It was the same scream I'd heard in fifth grade, when Rosie Graham dared us all to watch *Poltergeist* at her slumber party and some of us were *seriously* not ready for that demons-in-the-TV situation. It was the scream I knew from last year's school production of *Sweeney Todd*. It was the same scream I'd heard in seventh grade, after the Horseshoe Bay Hoedown, when Trevor Griffin got to second base with Allison Ayers. Even though we'd had it on good information that he'd been crushing on *my* friend.

Daisy.

That scream was Daisy, and it was coming from the direction of her locker, and I couldn't remember the last time I'd moved this quickly at school without a PE teacher's whistle in the background, egging me on.

A small crowd had gathered around her locker by the time I arrived. Daisy was at the center of it, shaking, her mascara making streaky raccoon tracks around her eyes. Lena was at her side, one arm over Daisy's shoulder in a gesture that was at once protective and comforting.

"What . . . ," I started to ask, but immediately trailed off because the "what" that it was, was starkly, glaringly obvious now that I was here, alongside the crowd, taking in the tableau of Daisy's locker with shock.

THE CURSE LIVES.

The words were bright red, lurid, scrawled in harsh, crude lettering. The letters themselves dripped, tracing trails like bloodstains down Daisy's locker door.

Another note, another mention of the curse. I caught Lena's eye, and she nodded, imperceptible to anyone else, but unmistakable to me. Once was a prank, maybe. Twice? This was . . . calculated. We couldn't have denied it if we'd wanted to.

There was no way Daisy still wanted to.

Was there?

Another quick glance at Lena told me everything I needed to know. Daisy wasn't going to let go of the Naming Day reenactment unless Ghostface from *Scream* himself showed up at her door.

Maybe not even then.

I pushed through the small throng. "Guys, give her some space." People hovered, morbidly curious. I turned to a few timid-looking freshmen. "Go get the janitor. And you"—I pointed to another cluster—"can maybe let the office know what happened?"

Reluctantly, the rubberneckers cleared away. Once the three of us were alone, I looked Daisy up and down. "Are you okay?"

Though teary and shaken, she nodded. She did look okay— physically. But clearly still coming to terms with whoever had done this, and why. "Just freaked out." She sniffed.

"With good reason." I looked at the writing, so dark and accusing. "That's not—it isn't *blood*, is it?"

Lena ran an index finger through it, leaving a deep smudge. "Lipstick. Tom Ford, actually. I used to wear the same shade. Whoever did this has relatively high-end taste and didn't mind sparing the good stuff."

I slapped her lightly. "Never touch a crime scene." My friends knew better than that by now.

"It's not a *crime scene*," Daisy protested. "I mean, let's not overreact." She folded her arms over her chest and looked at me, pleading with me to see it her way.

Lena and I exchanged another look over Daisy's head. If Lena had been Team Daisy after the raven incident—or at least willing to give the whole situation a little more time to play out—she wasn't anymore.

"Babe," Lena said, adopting her no-nonsense, come-to-Jesus

tone that she saved for special occasions, "be reasonable. This totally *is* a crime scene. I mean, like, the literal definition of one. It's vandalism, if nothing else, which maybe isn't dangerous, but, like, I don't think it's great news."

"So someone was trying to freak me out, so what? We talked about this yesterday, with the whole raven thing," Daisy protested. "Pranks are just the usual around here. It's super NBD."

"Exactly. We talked about it *yesterday*, Dais," I said gently. "It's probably connected, and it's escalating. Don't you think that's a little weird? The 'whole raven thing' was pretty insane in the first place, like, just on its own. But when you add this to it? Honestly, Lena's right. It has to be more than just a harmless prank. It's bad news."

Daisy looked at me. "You think someone is trying to sabotage the reenactment?"

I gestured at the lipstick marks, so blaring and ugly. "What would you call that?"

"Amateur hour," she said. "That's what I'd call it. It's *not* a threat. And even if it were, I'm not easily intimidated."

I couldn't believe what I was hearing. "Clearly not." I didn't want to argue. But she was being unreasonable.

"Look, we know how excited you are about Naming Day," Lena chimed in. "We were too. But someone out there is less than thrilled."

"Maybe more than one someone," I put in. *Possibly Caroline.* But she wasn't a very strong candidate as a suspect. But that didn't mean I wouldn't keep her in mind. "And I think we have to pay attention to the message they're sending."

"They're sending a message? So let them!" Daisy said shrilly. "You sent those kids to tell the office about what happened, right? I mean, it's not a secret, the way—"

"—the way you asked us to keep the raven thing," I finished for her. "Yeah, I offered to back off of that one—a *little*. But given this . . . new development," I said, grasping for phrasing that would get my point across without making Daisy more upset than she already was, "I don't think I can just pretend that something fishy isn't going on. I wouldn't be a good friend if I could!" I touched her arm, aiming for soothing, but she flinched and pulled back.

"Just let the office investigate it, then," she said. She shrugged. "I mean, I know you legitimately *can't* do that. Like, you're physically incapable. I'm sure you weren't going to just *completely* let the whole thing with the raven go totally untouched." She arched an eyebrow, the effect all the more unnerving given her smeary eye makeup. She didn't seem angry, just resigned to how well she knew me. "Were you?"

I flushed. "You asked me not to alert anyone. I didn't alert anyone." Except for Ms. Beekman, of course, in a roundabout way . . . but given how she hadn't wanted to touch the topic with a ten-foot pole, I wasn't all that worried about her further spilling the beans.

"I'm not *not* gonna participate in the reenactment," Daisy said, jutting her chin at Lena and me, a defiant glint in her eye.

"And *I'm* not *not* gonna keep looking into this curse thing, and trying to keep you—and everyone else involved—safe," I countered.

"Wonderful," Lena said drily. "In the world of non-ideal scenarios, this is probably the best case I can think of." She glared at Daisy. "Better would be you using an ounce of self-preservation and common sense rather than letting your thirst for theatrics win out."

Daisy shot her a smug smile in return. "Never gonna happen. You know the prospect of my name in lights is going to triumph every time."

"Drama queen," I said, not without affection. Were we at an impasse or a détente? I wasn't sure, but it was better than straight-up arguing. My main priority, as I said, was looking into the history of the Naming Day curse while also keeping Daisy—and whoever else may have been a target of these so-called pranks—safe. I didn't mind if Daisy got annoyed with me in the process, but everything was certainly easier (and more fun, obviously) when we were getting along.

I gave her a quick squeeze that I hoped was reassuring. "We probably have a few minutes before anyone from the office comes to check this out. Or clean it up," I said, taking a few pictures with my phone for good measure, being sure to zoom in and out to get every possible angle and detail. "So let's go to the bathroom and splash some water on your face before they get here."

"Sounds good," Daisy said. She rubbed a finger under her eye and looked at the smudge of mascara that appeared. "I guess I need it."

"You do," Lena assured her. "A drama queen *and* a crybaby," she teased, prompting Daisy to give her a playful shove. "You really are the total package. No wonder Coop's so smitten." The two dissolved into giggles, and for a second, I might have even been able to pretend that things were totally normal and my friends and I *weren't* being stalked by freaks who thought dead birds and bloodred threats were high comedy.

But as we turned the corner to the girls' bathroom, I realized something.

Not *everyone* had dispersed when Lena and I had sent them away.

One person in particular had managed to shuffle just down the hall, wedging himself against a wall of lockers in exactly the position a person would need to be in if they wanted to keep an eye on Daisy in the aftermath of the locker prank. One person had taken it all in, for reasons I could only guess at—but that I couldn't imagine were good.

Theo.

And if he felt any guilt or self-consciousness as I passed him with my friends in the hallway, he didn't show it.

In fact, as I strode past him, my own face surely a question mark, he was so still, so unresponsive, that I had to wonder.

Where did Theo—a self-proclaimed anarchist—fit into all this?

CHAPTER EIGHT

Things were better with Daisy by the end of the day, but not so much better that she was totally cool with me heading off to do my own thing after the final bell rang.

"What do you mean, you aren't staying to work on the float?" she demanded as I did my best to say my good-byes and make a graceful exit in the student lounge.

"I think she means, *she isn't staying to work on the float*," Lena offered. "Did the lipstick fumes from that locker thing get to you?" I wanted to shoot her a grateful look, but her expression was totally inscrutable. Was she annoyed that I was bailing on our plans? Just one more unsolvable question.

Some mysteries were more fun than others. It was just part of the gig.

"I mean, that much I got," Daisy said. "Though the closed captioning is always appreciated."

It didn't *sound* particularly appreciated, I had to say.

"But *why*?" Daisy glared at me. "We planned this days ago. We always do the float together. Last year was pirates."

"I know," I said. "Yo ho ho. Good times." I tried to smile, but she wasn't having it.

"And this year, the mermaid theme? I mean, Nancy—that was totally your idea!"

"Mind you, maybe a slightly obvious choice, but she's not wrong," Lena said. "It was all you, sister."

"I *know*," I repeated, testier now but working really, really hard not to show it.

"So what is it, then, that's *so important* that you have to bail on the float today?" Daisy asked. She eyed me like she had an idea, but didn't go so far as to actually accuse me of anything specific.

"I have an errand," I hedged.

In my jacket pocket, my hand closed around my cell phone. What I *had*, more precisely, was a friend at city hall who owed me a favor—I'd found her lost cat years ago in one of my easier cases. And what *she* had was access to a wider database that would hopefully help me dig up the original article about the Naming Day curse from the *Tribune*.

She also had tipped me off that the records room employee had a habit of sneaking off early on weekdays, and I only had a small window before the building closed for the night. Hence, making the hard choices even though my two best friends were looking at me like I was an utter rat for cutting out on our plans.

"Look, you guys—you know I'll make it up to you. Save me

a job. I'll be there as soon as I can to get it done." I hoped that meant this afternoon, but there was no way to be sure, and making promises I couldn't possibly keep felt like a terrible tactic, all things considered.

"Oh, don't worry. We'll save you a job," Lena promised ominously. "It'll be an unpleasant one."

"I would expect nothing less."

Daisy gave me one last harrumph as we said our good-byes. She was tolerating me, but just barely.

Meanwhile, Lena linked an arm through my own and led me to the parking lot exit of the school. "Do I want to know more about this errand?" she asked, once we got there.

I glanced at her. "*Do* you?" I didn't think so.

She shrugged. "Plausible deniability is probably better for me."

What did I tell you?

"But, look—between us? I support whatever it is you're doing. I think Daisy's taken the Naming Day fever a little too far, and I'm worried." Lena *looked* worried too.

"Me too." It was a relief to be able to say it so plainly.

"So, you know—do what you gotta do, Drew." She smiled. "That rhymes."

"Cute. And it does take some of the sting out of the possible-impending-danger aspect of this whole thing."

"Eh." Lena shrugged again before turning to go. "If you're on the case, I'm not too worried," she tossed over her shoulder.

That makes one of us.

* * *

"Nancy!"

I was at my car, shoving books onto the passenger seat, when I heard my name. Not Lena or Daisy this time—they'd both be in the shop studio, working on the mermaid float by now. Possibly with Daisy finding the time to construct a voodoo doll in my image in a spare moment. The good news was, it was hard to find a match for the particular red shade of my hair. . . .

I turned. It was Parker. "Hey," I said, warmth flooding through me at the sight of him. His hair flopped over one eye, and he was slightly out of breath. He carried a soccer ball under one arm. Had he come running after me straight from gym class? I decided I liked him even better mildly disheveled.

Get your head out of the clouds and into the game, Drew.

Way easier said than done, with Parker standing in front of me, looking nervous.

"Hey," he finally replied. Then he reddened. "Sorry, that was uninspired."

"Don't beat yourself up," I teased. "Sometimes you've gotta stick with the classics."

"Are you not helping out with the mermaid float?" he asked. "I'd—well, I heard from Lena you were going to be there."

He'd *heard* I was going to be there? As in, he'd asked someone (Lena, apparently) whether or not that was true?

As in, he was asking questions about me?

The idea bubbled up inside me, delightful.

I'd known *I* was curious about Parker as soon as he'd noticed me pocketing that note from the raven's beak. It was exciting to know he was curious about me, too.

I had to wonder what about me, specifically, had piqued *his* interest.

Facts: yes.

Science: please.

Love: ask again later.

That was my philosophy, as per the Magic 8 Ball in my brain. My last epic crush, David Cates, had crashed and burned freshman year. It happened right after I'd uncovered his father's e-mail flirtations with our town's then-pharmacist. David had told me his dad was acting weird, but it turned out that he hadn't really meant it when he'd mused that he wanted to know why.

Let's just say I learned the hard way that curiosity kills more than the cat, to use the lovely Ms. Beekman's choice of cliché. Sometimes it also kills a burgeoning relationship.

Since then I've been a little more cautious about my crushes.

But—*crap*—it was my turn to talk, and here I was, stuck in my head, being all bubbly and swoony in a decidedly un-Nancy way.

"Um," I started, aiming for "smooth" and missing it by at least a mile. "I was. Going to be there," I stumbled. "But something came up." I flushed. "Are you? Going to be there, I mean?" *So, so far from smooth.*

"Well, yeah," he said, his eyes twinkling. "I have to admit, I'm a little nervous. I'm not exactly a natural with all those shop tools and things. I'm guessing there's a ninety percent chance I walk away from this thing with at least one less finger than I started with. Maybe ninety-five."

"Those odds are . . . not good," I laughed. "Why'd you volunteer, then? If it's not your thing? I mean—it's nice that you did," I added, seeing a brief look of confusion cross his face. "But I just meant that there are other ways of helping. That don't involve . . . power tools and potentially severed extremities. There's always a bake sale. For instance. Very little personal disfigurement involved in the bake sale."

"Oh, but see—I'm special," Parker said. "I'm *definitely* likely to do just as much damage in the kitchen as I am with a buzz saw. Maybe more. Microwave pizza is as far as my culinary skills go."

"You can use store-bought," I teased. "It's frowned upon, but I won't tell."

"Yeah." He looked at me, direct and unwavering. "You do seem like the kind of girl who knows how to keep a secret. That's a compliment, by the way."

"Thank you, by the way," I said, that bubbly feeling stretching all the way to my toes. "I am." If he only knew.

"It was for you," he blurted suddenly, abrupt. His cheeks flamed red again, and he ran a hand through his hair, looking intensely anxious all of a sudden.

"What was?" I'd been too focused on the bubbles in my stomach—and the twinkle in his eyes—and I'd missed some key moment in the conversation, obviously.

"I mean, I'd heard you were working on the float. From Lena. It's why *I* volunteered to work on the float."

"Oh," I stumbled, mildly (but pleasantly) taken aback. *Oh.*

"Yeah, 'oh,'" he said. "And here I had to psych myself up for the whole working-with-power-tools thing just to get a chance to spend some time with this mysterious girl from the newspaper . . . and then it turns out she's blowing it off."

"I promise it's for a good reason," I insisted, hoping more than ever that was true. For once, the prospect of a mystery had the slightest twinge of obligation. "And—bonus! Now you probably won't lose a thumb today."

"Nah, I'll still go and help out," he said, stuffing his hands into his pocket. "I signed up and everything, I can't just bail now that the gorgeous, mysterious girl is mysteriously otherwise occupied."

"I'm . . . glad to see you have enough guilt about it for the both of us?" Of course, his level of guilt being so high meant mine was probably lower than it should be. But if I could uncover even one single, concrete fact about this curse, it would be worth it.

Right?

Also? It did not escape my attention that he'd called me "gorgeous."

Looking at Parker's face, playfully disappointed, a date with a contact at town hall suddenly felt like a terrible use of time.

"I'm a very responsible person," he said. "So responsible, in fact, that I feel like we should arrange right now to meet up later, just so that I can be sure you make it back from this secret mission—"

"*Errand*," I corrected. He didn't need to know the details about my penchant for deep-cover investigation.

"Mission, errand, whatever. I just want to be sure you make it back in one piece."

I tried to play suave. "How very gallant," I said, hoping he couldn't hear the slight tremor in my voice. "I can . . . text you? Tonight?"

"Texting is fine, I suppose," he said. "But 'gallant' is more than a text. 'Gallant' is maybe a snack and some face time. Like, say . . . at the Claw? Maybe around six?"

One by one, the bubbles in my stomach popped . . . with glee, and something more difficult to define. My insides were goo, and my throat was filled with butterflies. But somehow, the cumulative sensation of it all was *amazing*.

"A date," I said cautiously. The prospect was heady. Was it a good idea to be going on dates when there was a possibly dangerous mystery in the air? Maybe not. But looking at Parker, I wasn't sure how to resist. This was the guy who'd witnessed my sleight of hand and called me out on it too, where most guys I'd dated were more annoyed by my detective skills than anything else. That felt different. Maybe even dangerous? Promising, but also scary.

Dates were fine. Fun, even. But this was something new. Something that might be more than just casual fun. Something that could be a distraction.

And a sleuth on a case can't always afford a distraction.

"It doesn't have to be a date," Parker said, reading the ambivalence on my face. "It can just be . . . a bite to eat? I'll make sure your secret mission went off without a hitch; you'll check me for grievous bodily harm. And if things start to feel date-like . . . well, we can put a stop to that nonsense right away, should it feel necessary." He tilted his head. "What do you say?"

I had to laugh. "Well, as long as there's a contingency plan in place. In case things get too romantic." My cell phone, still in my jacket pocket, buzzed, snapping me back to reality and reminding me that I *did* actually have a secret mission to get to.

"I have to run," I said reluctantly. "But yes. I'll see you at the Claw. Six." It was only a few hours away, but I knew it would feel like so much more.

"Every good love story starts with a solid plan B," he said. I tried not to shiver at the words "love story." "See you then."

CHAPTER NINE

Horseshoe Bay City Hall. Like so much of our town, it was a building straight from a Norman Rockwell painting: faded, sun-bleached brick, Grecian columns flanking the entrance, and a jaunty turret standing tall against the cloudless blue sky. The salt air had scarred the clapboard shingles a weathered hue that stood stark and gray against the seascape backdrop that surrounded it.

It was *also* possibly my last hope for finding any information about the history of the Naming Day curse.

Not to put too *much pressure on this mission or anything.*

I checked my watch: 4:13 p.m. My contact had told me that while city hall *officially* closes at four thirty on weekdays, the records room was managed by a cranky septuagenarian game show enthusiast, who unfailingly raced home at three forty-five every day to catch *Supermarket Sweep* in syndication. And while

I wondered why he was so resistant to the age of streaming, I had to admit that his old-school ways were *extremely* helpful to my investigation.

Walking in the front door was out of the question—the receptionist knew my parents and would have recognized me in a heartbeat. I wasn't doing anything wrong, but I didn't need any questions or interference from authority figures. Luckily, the side door was unguarded. (Small-town life could often be charmingly, misguidedly trusting, but just this once, I wasn't complaining.) A quick glance over my shoulder told me I wasn't being watched, and given that no one had any idea I was even looking into the curse, why would anyone have been watching? But still: I was always thankful for small favors and all that. I turned the door handle.

Locked.

Okay, small-ish hitch. But only *ish*. After all, I'd been picking locks since I was seven. I pulled my lockpick from the kit I kept in my bag, and with a few quick twists, the handle gave way and I was inside.

Another benefit of living in a small town was that our town hall, too, was relatively small. The records room was in the basement, just around one corner and down a hall and then a flight of stairs. I could hear footsteps at the front of the building—not everyone in the building was obsessed with the Game Show Network, clearly, which was sort of a relief, on a purely sociological level—but I slipped inside totally unnoticed.

And then my stomach dropped.

Because even if Horseshoe Bay was small, somehow, its history, when stacked file box on file box, row after row, shelf after shelf, looked absolutely endless. The section marked PERIODICALS towered against an entire wall, taller than I was. By a *lot*.

At least they're labeled.

As bright sides went, it was a reach.

The boxes were in alphabetical order: *Beacon, the Bangor*; *Chronicle, the Boston*; *Daily, the Montpelier . . . Tribune, the Horseshoe Bay* was a column of the wall unto itself, with the oldest papers lowest to the ground. I had to narrow down the time frame. But when had that one random online hit been from? Suddenly, my mind went blank. I pulled out my phone.

No service. Of course. Not even a broken link would be useful to me down here, in the bowels of this building.

Good thing I'd taken a quick snapshot of the original search results screen with my phone the other day.

Let's just say I'd learned the hard way the importance of covering one's bases.

I opened my photo album; the picture was one of the first images to come up. "A Blessing or a Curse?," a piece in the opinion section of the paper, though the name of the author wasn't listed in the heading. But the year was: 1971. *Bingo.*

Or . . . sort of "bingo." 1971 was only three boxes. *Great.* That would take . . . I didn't have the heart to do the math.

But no. The op-ed piece was about Naming Day, obviously, meaning it probably ran around the same time of the year. That further narrowed down the time window considerably.

Relieved, I pulled out the box that I needed, sneezing as a cloud of dust erupted with it. I pored through the paper-thin pages as quickly and gently as I could, mindful that age had made the newspapers fragile.

Twenty minutes later, and I had it. So much for fuzzy math; every now and then a girl got lucky. A 1971 issue of the *Tribune* with a teaser on its front page, "Longtime rez sees silver lining to so-called Naming Day curse," with a directive to "see page 13."

I flipped, trying to tamp down the eager curiosity building in me.

Slow and steady, girl.

It was a good call, not letting my enthusiasm run away with me. Because when I got to the page?

The article was missing.

Scratch "lucky," then.

Not the whole *page*, mind you. Apparently, whoever it was in this world that was either deliberately or inadvertently trying to sabotage me thought *that* would be overkill. No, only the bottom half of it was absent, excised so cleanly a person might have thought it was meant to be that way. If that person weren't me, on a tear, desperate to find the article in question.

I blinked, confused and unwilling to believe my own eyes. I rechecked the front page of the paper: *see page 13*. I looked again to the top right-hand corner of the page: *13*.

Definitely missing. And probably not by coincidence.

But . . . maybe it hadn't been removed that cleanly, after all.

An old-school detective might have used a magnifying

glass—think Sherlock Holmes, or Hercule Poirot. But this was the twenty-first century. I pulled out my smartphone.

The page had been sliced along the fold. At first glance—at *my* first glance, that was—it looked as though anything useful had been cut away.

Thank goodness *I* know better than to rely on first glances.

I clicked my camera and immediately blew the image up, fingers skating along the smooth glass of my phone screen. Slowly, shapes that had seemed like little more than random squiggles revealed themselves to be inside-out, fun-house reflections of letters. It took me a moment to piece them together into something whole in my brain.

S-T-R-A-T-H-M-O-R-E.

It wasn't an obvious word, nothing I—or anyone else—would have guessed. But that was okay. Because I'd been doing this for long enough. It wasn't an *obvious* word—it was a surname.

The surname of the person who'd written the piece.

Here were the facts:

First, a total lack of online footprint. Then, a missing hard copy in the official city hall record. Someone out there sure didn't want anyone reading this article. I was going to find out why. This partial byline—just a last name, and who knew if it would yield anything more than my first online search had—was a small lead. A minuscule clue, at best.

But I'd solved cases with less to go on. A lot less.

I rolled the ancient, ruined newspaper into a slim tube, gentle as ever with the crackly material. Then I slipped it carefully into my messenger bag, replaced the boxes I'd been digging through, and retraced my steps, up and out of the building, back into the waning sun of the early evening.

I'd been so busy keeping an eye out for any adults who might be keeping eyes on *me*, it somehow didn't even occur to me to be on the lookout for other high school students my own age.

"Caroline!" I literally walked directly into her, slamming against her with enough force to send us both rocking back. She, too, had her school bag with her, and she looked flustered from the impact.

"What the hell?" she asked, looking genuinely irked. I didn't blame her. "I know you and your friends think the world revolves around you, but you could maybe try not to walk directly *through* other people, you know."

"Sorry, I was—distracted. And I *don't* think the world revolves around me." She gave me a look that told me my protests were pointless.

"What are you doing here?" I said, forging ahead. Just outside of town hall, I meant, which wasn't exactly a high school hangout. But I could see where, from her point of view, it was exactly none of my business what she was doing walking around on a public street on a random Tuesday evening.

She looked at me like I was out of my mind. Or, maybe more precisely, like I was sticking my nose into things that were exactly none of my business. "Walking down Main Street, just like you are."

I held my hands up—*hey, no trouble here.* "Fair. Never mind."

She rolled her eyes. Still salty; I guessed she hadn't yet gotten over not being cast in the Naming Day reenactment. Though, given recent events, it felt like she should honestly be considering herself lucky.

And speaking of . . . Caroline's had been the first name to come up after the first note was found. Or, at least, the second name, after Theo managed to convince us he was way too much of a slacker to ever pull off anything so elaborate as that little number. But I hadn't had the chance to interrogate—I mean ask—her about it yet.

She was scowling at me, though. "If you have something to ask me, Nancy, just go for it."

O . . . kay. Cutting straight to the chase. I liked it; it made things easier. "I mean . . . as long as you brought it up."

She sighed heavily.

"I *was* wondering if you were anywhere on the school premises on Monday afternoon . . . say, around the time the *Masthead* was meeting?"

She raised an eyebrow. "And I suppose you were *also* wondering if I had anything to do with your girl Daisy's locker today. That whole 'curse' vandalism thing."

Okay, you got me. I had to admit, I was surprised she'd preempted my questions. At my curious look, she went on. "Lena 'talked' to me. After school today." The emphasis she placed on the word "talked" wasn't lost. I doubted it was a light, casual chat.

Oh. "Okay," I said. "I didn't know that."

"Oh, please," she scoffed.

It was hard to blame her for being disbelieving. "I swear," I said, trying to infuse my voice with as much sincerity as possible. "I had no idea. Although it does make sense, now that you mention it." As much as any of this made sense, which, of course, wasn't saying that much.

"*Not* that it's any of your business," she said, eyes flashing, "but I'll tell you what I told Lena. As it happens, I *was* at school on Monday afternoon, working on a paper in the library. And on Tuesday, I was with a teacher."

"Okay." I waited. I had a sense there was more to it, and that she was about to share—however resentfully.

"I was with Mr. Stephenson." She put a hand on her hip, daring me to challenge her.

She made it sound so certain, like this was the definitive be-all and end-all of the conversation. I wished I could see it that way. On the one hand, a person definitely wouldn't have had to be physically near the office to send that raven on its way . . . but on other hand, it was a seriously bold move to invoke a teacher's name the way Caroline had, in that, as alibis went, it was eminently verifiable. Not to mention, she *hadn't* mentioned a raven, which a guilty person might do to specifically refute their involvement, if he or she were trying to distance themselves from such a bizarre, specific action.

"You can ask him if you want." Caroline was still looking at me, waiting on a more dramatic reaction, I guessed.

I tried to look casual, though of course, of *course* I was

definitely going to do just that, as soon as I had a chance. "Okay," I said. "But you know that even if he verifies your alibi for Tuesday—"

"Oh, now it's an *alibi* that needs to be *verified*?" she asked, raising her voice.

Now *I* sighed. "What do you want me to say, Caroline? Something weird happened. You definitely already know that, because apparently Lena approached you about it. It sounds like she wasn't super nice either. And whatever she said, it made enough of an impression on you that you assumed I'd have questions of my own."

"It did." Her voice was tight. "And here you are. Look at that."

"I've definitely been called worse things than 'predictable.' Look, Caroline, you say you were with Mr. Stephenson on Tuesday? I'm inclined to believe you. As alibis go, it's one that's too easy to verify—or debunk—as I mentioned. But that doesn't account for what happened during the newspaper meeting. As you must know, someone vandalized Daisy's locker sometime today. And even if you *didn't* pull the locker prank, the *Masthead* incident definitely could have been you."

"How could that have been me? Or are you planning to question the entire student body?" Caroline asked.

Point.

But: counterpoint. "Daisy's my best friend. Do you really need to ask? If I have to, I will. But for now, I think I'll settle for the kids who have motives for wanting to take the reenactment down." I arched an eyebrow of my own. "Like you."

She swallowed, the spring breeze brushing her hair back from her face. "Look, I know I freaked out in the quad after the cast list was posted."

"That was more than just a 'freak-out,'" I said. "If I recall, it was a breakdown that required intervention from Stephenson himself."

"Okay, whatever. It was a total meltdown. I'm not gonna argue with you about what to call it. And yeah, I was disappointed, big-time. I expected to be cast. The reenactment show is a huge thing around here. I mean, what else do we even have going on in this Podunk town?"

"I happen to like this Podunk town," I replied, realizing as I said it that it was an easy claim to make, knowing I had an application to Columbia University just waiting to be filled out next year.

Caroline softened at that. "I do too," she admitted. "I guess making fun of Naming Day is just my way of pretending like it's no big deal I'm not gonna get to participate in the way I was hoping. You have to get it, right? I mean, I know you're, like, 'in'"—she made little air quotes with her fingers—"but those of us who are out? Well, we really feel it."

It was hard not to sympathize with her when she said that. I gave her a small smile. "If you're trying to play it cool, I get it. But I feel like the cat's maybe out of the bag by this point. I think people have the idea that you're upset. Or that you were." I held my breath: Would she be offended? I was trying to tease, but if Caroline had proven anything about herself recently, it was that with the right provocation, she could be easily triggered.

For a moment, her face was impassive, and I worried I'd set our conversation back at least fifty proverbial paces. But then, miraculously, she broke into a smile of her own. "Burn," she said, nodding appreciatively. "I like it."

Unexpected, but I'll take it.

"I don't blame you for suspecting me," Caroline said. She shrugged, looking resigned. "Honestly, I'd be surprised if you didn't. And, like I said, talk to Stephenson. He can tell you, at least, that I was with him on Tuesday. As for the *Masthead* thing? I don't know, I guess you'll have to decide whether or not to take my word for it."

"I can't promise I'm not going to do any more digging," I said.

"Again: unsurprising," Caroline said. "Your reputation precedes you as much as anyone's does."

"Well, sure," I said. "In a town like this, whose doesn't?"

CHAPTER TEN

In the short time I had to spare between bumping into Caroline and meeting Parker at the Claw, I managed to catch what was maybe the first break I'd had since I started investigating the Naming Day curse. Which was to say, when I googled *Strathmore*, I found more than one hit, but only one of a person: Glynnis Strathmore, who could plausibly have written an op-ed piece in 1971, who was also currently still living within ten miles of Horseshoe Bay, in the nearby hamlet of Stone Ridge.

I'd driven through Stone Ridge on family vacations to Shadow Ranch—before solving a mystery there had rendered it yet another awkward place for our little family to spend our free time—but I'd never stopped in. Still, though, this hit, this lead—it felt promising. I had that little hum in my blood that told me I was on the right track. Over the years, I'd learned well enough not to ignore that hum.

Whatever superstitions had inspired Glynnis Strathmore to write an opinion piece on the Naming Day curse, she wasn't so paranoid that her phone number didn't come up online right away. I dialed it eagerly from my bedroom, feeling grateful that my parents' work kept them occupied enough that I had way more privacy and independence than your average teenage girl. It wasn't something I took for granted.

She sounded surprised to hear from me, but I took it as being more surprised to hear from *anyone* than from me in particular, which was mildly heartbreaking. I mentioned the op-ed and she seemed stunned that anyone had stumbled across it. "That was so long ago, dearie," she said, her voice shaky with age. But she was perfectly happy to tell me more about it. "It's probably better if we meet in person, though" was her one caveat.

"Are you . . . Is privacy an issue?" She didn't strike me as someone who'd be very concerned with phone taps and stuff like that, what with being so very findable online. But I guessed even that blood hum I get can occasionally be wrong, especially when it comes to the tin hat brigade. You never do know what specifically is going to set someone off.

"I assure you, I'm very discreet," I went on. "I'm just curious. About the piece you wrote, anything you might know about the curse. I'm covering the Naming Day reenactment for the Horseshoe Bay *Masthead*, and I stumbled on a few mentions of it. But only a very few. No one seems to know anything about it, and I was wondering what the story was there."

There was a burst of static at the other end of the phone,

followed by a snort of laughter. "Privacy? Heavens, no," she said, barely able to contain herself. "Certainly I'm of no interest to anyone important out there. There's nothing to be so private about. It's only that the backstory to the curse is one of those stranger-than-fiction sort of deals. And, like you said, no one *does* seem to mention it nowadays—I suppose people prefer their curses connected to sexy vampires or zombies, like those loud TV shows on the cable—"

"Well, I can't say I'm all that important, but I for one would love to hear what you have to say," I cut in, hoping to head off a long, rambling diatribe on the current state of pop culture, about which, even within the short few minutes since we'd been speaking, Ms. Strathmore had already made her opinions clear.

"Why don't you come here, then?" she suggested, and the hope in her voice was almost more than I could bear. "You say you're in Horseshoe Bay; that's not terribly far."

"Not far at all," I agreed. "Is there a time that works best for you?"

"Oh, heavens—my schedule's quite open," she said, snort-laughing again with gusto. "Retirement, you know. Twenty-two years on the school board—"

"Well, how about"—I glanced at my watch—"half an hour? It shouldn't take me longer than that to get myself together and drive over." I'd heard all about her years teaching first grade. Honestly, we'd covered a startling amount of ground in the short time since I'd called her. This was a woman who was *thrilled* to have someone to talk to.

And I was all ears. It would mean pushing Parker back a little bit, but I could do it.

We confirmed her address, and I plugged it into my phone's GPS. Whoever it was that had ripped her piece from the official city hall records of the *Horseshoe Bay Tribune* had obviously not counted on a twenty-first-century teenage girl and her trusty smartphone.

I love being underestimated.

Nancy: Hey, quick favor: Any chance you can meet closer to 8 p.m.? Something came up.

Parker: You sure? If you need to reschedule, it's no problem.

Parker: I mean, sure, my pride will be wounded beyond all repair, but, like, other than that, no problem at all.

Nancy: The last thing I'd want to do would be to wound your pride, clearly. But even if you weren't such a clearly fragile flower, I promise—I want to see you. I just have some stuff to take care of.

Parker: As long as you're sure. I mean, I can't help but notice that 8 p.m. is dangerously close to what some might consider a more traditionally date-like hour. Harder to play things off as super casual, come 8 p.m.

Nancy: I'll take my chances.

Parker: I love a girl with a sense of adventure.

Though it wasn't far at all from Horseshoe Bay, the short geographic distance to Stone Ridge spanned huge gaps just in terms of topography. As I drove, dune brush gave way to pine trees, and the roads grew thick and wooded. Pine needles covered the roads rather than sand, and the ocean salt in the air faded until all I could smell was crisp evergreen growth.

If I'd googled *Maine retiree, home environment,* the house at the end of the drive I was currently pulling up to would have been the photo to accompany the Wikipedia entry I turned up. I was also getting the *slightest* tinge of "murderer's cabin in the woods" from Glynnis's driveway, but I was doing my best to push those thoughts out of my mind as I twisted along the tree-lined path, braked, and killed the ignition.

Glynnis's home was a modest cottage, a sturdy one-level cabin built from dark logs and adorned with chalet-style red shutters. Window boxes were planted with bright yellow marigolds, despite the fact that the season was almost over. Whoever this woman was and whatever her backstory, she clearly took a lot of pride and pleasure in her home, even if it wasn't big or flashy. The yellow of the flowers and the red of the shutters went a long way toward undoing the creepy horror-movie vibe that came over me as I'd first turned down the drive.

I'll take it.

The door swung open away from me just as I raised my finger to ring the bell, telling me that Glynnis had already been poised directly on the other side of it, waiting. While her enthusiasm for my visit was great news for the investigation, every cell of her being screamed *loneliness.* It made me feel slightly uncomfortable about the self-serving nature of my visit. But not uncomfortable enough to turn around and go home.

"Hello, dearie," she said, smiling over a pair of embellished mother-of-pearl glasses that on someone twenty years younger would have been the height of geek chic. "Please do come in."

She ushered me into a living room that felt like a time capsule: frilly chintz upholstery cased in plastic slipcovers that squeaked awkwardly as I settled myself on a small sofa, setting my bag beside me. The space felt a little lonely, desolate, but quiet and harmless. "Thank you so much for agreeing to speak with me, Ms. Strathmore," I said.

"Of course. Happy to do it. As you've probably guessed, I don't get too many visitors these days."

"That's a shame," I said, meaning it. "Do you—ah, I normally take notes, and record my interviews. Would that be okay?" I pulled out my leather notebook and set my phone to record.

She frowned for a moment, like she was considering it. Her white hair hung in tight corkscrews that bobbed with her every movement. "I don't see why not."

Really? The total lack of information available—and the fact that someone had gone to pretty decent lengths to hide the information that *was* available in the first place—said otherwise.

I hesitated, unsure whether to mention that it had literally been pulled from the official records. I decided to wait. I didn't want to risk spooking her now and accidentally creating an abrupt ending to our meeting.

"Oh!" Her eyes flashed with realization. "I almost forgot. I baked cookies."

Of course she had. Now that she mentioned it, though, I could smell the sugar and spice in the air.

"I hope you like oatmeal raisin," she said, bustling through a low doorway into what was obviously the kitchen.

"It's my favorite," I said, which wasn't strictly true, but in this case, a white lie was harmless enough.

"And some tea?" she called. "The water's just boiled. I have mint and chamomile."

"Um, mint, please," I said.

"Sugar?"

"No, thank you," I called back, beginning to feel slightly fidgety. Glynnis Strathmore clearly did not share my personal sense of urgency.

After a moment, she came back into the room, this time carrying a silver tray with a platter of the oatmeal cookies and a small tea set: a pot, two teacups and saucers, and tiny spoons. She set the entire platter on the polished mahogany coffee table, poured me a mug of tea from the pot, and sat back into an armchair catty-corner to me, folding her arms across her chest.

"Now, then," she said, taking a generous bite out of one of the cookies, spraying a fine layer of crumbs down the front of her popcorn-knit sweater, "you had questions about the Naming Day curse."

"I did, yes." Ready to get down to business, I tucked my hair behind my ear and replaced the cup of tea with my notebook and pen. "Mostly, I'm just interested in the details. The actual origin story. What *is* the curse?"

"I'm certain you know more than you think you do," she said, looking wistful for a moment. "The Naming Day curse is really just one of so many ghoulish legends on which Horseshoe Bay was first founded."

I shivered. "But you're saying this one, at least, isn't *just* a legend."

She nodded. "That's precisely what I'm saying.

"Horseshoe Bay has a bloody backstory," Glynnis said, startling me out of my reverie. "Perhaps you can even recall when you first heard some variation on one of its more ghastly history lessons."

I thought for a beat. Images flashed: Fourth of July fireworks celebrations. Mayoral parades. Slumber parties. Campouts. Whispers throughout them all, grown-ups and children alike. But I actually couldn't think of when I'd heard of a specific Naming Day curse.

I pushed the phone closer to Glynnis as she went on. "This one begins like any other. Naming Day celebrates the town's roots. But the town's roots were, in fact, slow to take hold. The first winter settling Horseshoe Bay was difficult. Food was scarce, and deaths were plentiful. The cold was bitter and unforgiving. The settlers persevered, though, and through some minor miracle, they survived to see spring."

Spring. Hope. All things bright and optimistic. Why did I suspect spring hadn't been so shiny and hopeful in this story?

"A celebration was planned, the youths of the town set to prepare a performance, right on the bluff overlooking the magnificent bay. They'd been preparing for weeks. But when the day of the performance arrived, the actors were . . . missing."

"Missing?" I swallowed.

She nodded. "Indeed. As time passed and no one showed, a crisis was declared. Search parties combed the bluffs, and the surrounding forests, but the children had vanished without a trace."

"*Nothing* was found?"

"Not a scrap of clothing, nor a single footprint."

My throat felt tight. This was all very "Roanoke." How was it possible for a group of people to disappear into thin air?

"As you can imagine, hysteria ensued."

"Nobody likes an unsolved mystery," I said. *Least of all, me.*

"Indeed. People claimed that the town was cursed. The town leaders, in an effort to quell the panic, were quick to point a finger. A man was convicted purely on speculation." She narrowed her gaze. "Humanity's always been superstitious at heart."

It's always a sacrifice.

"They all stood by to watch," Glynnis said. "When they strung him from the hanging tree."

"Who was it?" I was practically holding my breath.

It was always a sacrifice, it was always a curse. That was the story, right? Of history? Of men, conquering. Something—some*one*—had to be conquered in the process.

"No one knows. These days, there are just theories among us history buffs. But it seems that it was a member of a prominent family. The more scandal, the more eager people were to believe it, so it goes."

The clink of her setting her teacup on the table made me flinch.

"This town does love its ghost stories," I said. I didn't expect it would lighten the mood, really—Glynnis had already indicated that now that the cookies and tea were out of the way and we were on to the meat of the story, there would be no further lightening. It was more that I had to balance my need to keep her talking with my own need to push back against any suggestion that the supernatural—a *curse*, no less—could be real. "What made them suspect . . . whoever it was?"

"It was a girl, of course," Glynnis said.

It was always a girl. That, too, was perennial in the history of men and conquest.

"Legend tells he was in love with one of the performers, but she spurned his advances."

"So he killed her, and made her disappear. Along with the rest of the performers." It was elaborate . . . but as a detective, I knew that people had done even worse, for even less.

Who needs a curse when we have real-life monsters in the mix?

I shivered. I couldn't help myself. The sun was setting beyond the living room window, fiery and fierce. Had the temperature dropped in this room since I'd arrived? It felt that way, but Glynnis's expression remained fixed, impassive. "You know what comes next," she said, prompting me, almost goading me. "Or you can guess. You're a sharp one. I can see it in your eyes."

"The festival," I said automatically. "They held it anyway."

"Yes. So they hung the man in the center of the town square. Everyone came out to watch. Days later, a new show was performed: this one, a reenactment like the one the children put on to this very day."

I looked at Glynnis, held her gaze. "This is an awful story. But I don't believe in curses."

"Of course, you're right. Neither do I. And we do commemorate those settlers every year, so clearly, whatever they may or may not have done—whoever it was—it hasn't tarnished their reputations. Not to any notable degree."

I exhaled, only semisurprised not to see my own breath curl out into the air in front of me like a plume of smoke. It *was* colder in that cabin, I was sure of it, though Glynnis had been sitting with me since she'd first brought in the tea tray and there was no reasonable explanation as to why the temperature in the room should have dropped.

I heard a sharp *crack* and jumped in my seat.

"Tense, sweetheart?" Glynnis observed, watching me flush and settle back against the rubbery cover of her couch. The squeak of the plastic was damning.

"I . . . the window. I thought I heard something," I said, embarrassed. *Keep it together, Drew.*

"The wind can be strong here in the woods," she said. "It was likely just a branch. You get used to the sounds of nature."

I was sure she was right. But it had been barely a day since the last smashed window—and the blown-out light!—in my life, and that one hadn't been something innocent or ignorable. *So you'll forgive me for being jumpier than usual.*

"You must get your own fair share of . . . *ambient noise*, being on the ocean." She took a sip of her own tea, the rattle of the cup against its saucer making me think of chattering teeth.

"At a certain point you stop hearing it. It doesn't register. The sound of the ocean just turns into white noise," I told her.

"I remember. It seems a shame, in a way, to come to take something like that for granted. But you're not wrong." At my questioning glance, she reminded me, "I did live there once. As you must know, if you found that piece—found *me*—in the first place." She looked at the window, at the spot where that one thick, crooked branch still scratched against the glass, evaluating. "To be perfectly frank, I didn't find the ocean sounds to be soothing, though. Something about the call of the gulls."

"What was it?" I asked, flashing back to the image of inky feathers beating against my flesh.

"To me, it always sounded like screaming."

I could hear it too—a thin, reedy keening in the distance, like the wail of a dying animal. Was I imagining things? Like the chill in the air, it was hard to prove but even harder to ignore.

I was officially creeped out. And that's not something that happens often.

It must have shown on my face—apparently I was doing a lousy job of concealing my reactions today—because she brusquely sat up in her chair again. "But you were asking about my piece. About the Naming Day curse. And I'm sorry to say, there aren't too many details to be added."

"To your article?" I asked, confused.

"To the curse itself," she said. "That was the crux of my article in the first place: how much Horseshoe Bay loves its traditions, but how arbitrary so many of them are. I argued that the Naming

Day curse is yet another example of, as you call it, small-town mythology, and no one actually knows the specific origins of it. Somewhat of a 'blessing,' as the article termed my letter. Here we are, inspired every year to reexamine the sins of our fathers— quite literally, in this case. Even without a true origin story." She laughed. "We're reminded of the evil that man is capable of."

"I'm amazed you were able to dig up any information on the curse in the first place."

She looked at me. "I'm a smart one too." She leaned forward, peering at me. "And though it's not something I like to revisit, the fact is that it's because of the article that I relocated to Stone Ridge. There were people in Horseshoe Bay who weren't happy to have me stirring up ancient history."

I shuddered. The idea that this woman had been forced to move based on a piece she'd written criticizing the town's history? I needed all the info. I had to come clean. There was no option, at this point. "The truth is, Ms. Strathmore—"

"Glynnis," she corrected.

"*Glynnis.* The truth is, I didn't read the article. I couldn't, actually."

"Then how did you find me?" she asked.

"I *saw* it. The title of the article came up in an online search. But the link didn't lead anywhere. So I went to town hall to check in the back issues of the *Tribune*. And I found it there."

"But you didn't read it? If I may say so—that doesn't seem like you. You strike me as the type who does her homework."

"Well, no. I mean, yes, I am the type who does her homework.

I guess what I mean is, I found the paper where your piece ran. But the article itself . . . it was gone. Someone took it."

She furrowed her brow. "Took it? Well, I suppose it's like I've been saying—people don't want to confront the uncomfortable truths. If they were willing to chase me out of town, practically wielding pitchforks, is it any wonder they'd destroy what little evidence remains about the curse in the first place?"

I shivered again, and not only because of the chill in the room. "No," I said. "It's no wonder at all."

CHAPTER ELEVEN

What was that line from that movie, again? The one with the police lineup and the big twist ending with the guy with the limp? *The greatest trick the Devil ever pulled was convincing the world he didn't exist.*

So the Naming Day curse was probably just another tall tale, like Bloody Mary or the Easter Bunny, told to keep children in line and later just from sheer force of folk nostalgia or habit.

And yet.

Someone out there felt strongly enough about this imaginary curse to try and erase that one, singular mention. The person who'd written the piece had been tormented, ostracized, and run out of town. The hard copy had been destroyed, and I didn't doubt for a minute that whoever had been invested enough in disappearing the article could have also done a little digital scrubbing, either on their own or with some generous funding.

But *why?*

The question rattled through me as my car bumped along the wooded path leading from Ms. Strathmore's cabin. The moon was out now, a small slash set against a blaze of stars.

It *was* cold out here, colder than nights by the bay had been lately, and I'd cranked the heat as soon as my car had warmed up enough. Now the windows were fogging over slightly, which wasn't great given that even *with* clear windows, visibility out here in the woods was not the best. I hit the defroster button and clicked the windshield wipers on to clear the glass off.

And gasped.

Before the wipers cleaned away any trace, I saw a word written in the condensation: BEWARE.

But there hadn't been anyone around in the forest, other than Ms. Strathmore herself, either. It was so still, so quiet, it had almost freaked me out when I first pulled up at her cabin. We were alone.

Weren't we?

And wasn't I, still? Reflexively, I checked my rearview mirror. Then I nearly skidded off the road.

A pair of ghostly white legs dangled in the frame, streaked with mud.

I slammed on the brakes, sending the car skidding. I swerved to avoid a looming tree and clutched at the steering wheel, my heart thudding.

I had to check. I had to look and see. I had to know that whatever that was . . .

It had to be gone.

Slowly, I peeled my eyes open. I glanced at the windshield, feeling a trickle of sweat down the back of my neck.

The image had disappeared. Instead, there were two vines hanging down the back of my car, pieces of forest that must have fallen while I spoke with Glynnis. Who had been quite the story-teller, apparently, if her tale had me hallucinating like I just had.

I took a breath. It was just me, alone, in the forest, my pulse pounding and my heart in my throat.

And a sneaking sensation of being watched.

With Glynnis's words echoing in my head, dread settled over my shoulders as I cranked on the high beams, put the car back into drive, and screeched off down the road, away from the forest and back toward Horseshoe Bay, as fast as I possibly could.

The drive back felt much longer than the way to Ms. Strathmore's cabin. Normally, the reverse was true. But normally, I didn't have the sinking, suffocating feeling that I was being followed as I twisted my way down once-familiar, now-ominous roads. WELCOME TO HORSESHOE BAY, the sign read, but instead of relief at seeing it, my breath caught. A pair of twin beams appeared on the road behind me as I made a left turn onto Main Street. . . . Nothing particularly odd about that . . . except that literally moments before, the streets had been deserted. To the point that it had felt eerie to me.

Was I losing my mind? Clinging to the lingering aftereffects of whatever semibreakdown I'd had leaving Stone Ridge? It wasn't an appealing thought.

Casting a quick look in my side mirror, I pulled a left turn, sharp and abrupt. Now I'd have to make an unnecessary loop just to get to the Claw to meet Parker . . . but I *also* wasn't being maybe-followed anymore either.

With shock, I realized those twin beams appeared in my rearview mirror again, this time a few more paces back, rolling smoothly down the road. One of the headlights—the right one—flickered on and off like a stutter, then settled back into bearing down on me in tandem with the left again.

I squinted, ignoring the goose bumps breaking out on my forearms, trying to make out the car's license plate, but its headlights were too strong. Images from the past few days came to me, unbidden: Daisy's locker, trashed. The dead raven, its open, unseeing eye. The constant beating of feathers from my nightmare.

A deathly pale ankle, swaying slightly in the wind.

The Claw's sign beamed like a beacon, and I gratefully turned right, into the parking lot. It, too, was unusually empty—it was like the entire greater Horseshoe Bay environs had banded together to unsettle me.

It was working.

Shaking, I parked the car and killed the ignition, suddenly fearful of what I might see in my mirror if I dared look.

I dared. And there it was: a flash of headlights. As though whoever had been following me was still on my tail. *Even though I wasn't moving anymore.*

I blinked, terrified. When I opened my eyes again, the night was finally, blissfully still.

"Hey!"

I screamed.

"Sorry!" His voice was muffled through the car window, but it was clearly Parker, looking truly apologetic, his expression abashed and his hands up.

I opened the car door, humiliated, willing my pulse back down to its normal rate. "God, no—I'm sorry. I'm just . . . never mind. It's been a long night." I managed a small smile. "And it's barely eight o' clock."

"The witching hour," Parker joked, but I must have made a face at that, because he quickly changed tack. "Or—just as scary, to some—*dating* hour."

"Right, that." I smiled again, for real this time, beginning to feel some semblance of normalcy return. "You startled me. I overreacted. Let's start again."

"Happy to," Parker said, giving me a funny little bow. "Glad to see you. Hey, how are you? Sorry for sneaking up on you like that." He peered at me. "You were really shaken. I *am* sorry."

"You don't need to apologize," I assured him, following him toward the front door of the restaurant. "You didn't sneak up on me."

But he had, I realized as we walked through the door, overhead bell chiming our entrance. He absolutely had, which was kind of hard to believe, given that I was on extra-high alert and sitting in a wide-open parking lot, as one hundred percent focused on my immediate surroundings as a person could possibly be.

And, not to be too easily impressed with myself or anything, but, like, as a general rule, I tended to think of myself as someone who was difficult to catch off guard. So what did it mean, then, that Parker had done so—pretty impressively, at that?—in a moment when I'd like to think I was trying to be *hyper* vigilant?

The investigator in me, the one who was so wedded to facts they practically shared a surname, knew that it had to be one of two things:

Either I was woefully less alert tonight than I meant to be, which felt like exceedingly bad news, given how the night had been going. Or:

Parker had *meant* to startle me. He'd been trying, for some unfathomable reason, to sneak up on me.

The door to the Claw swung shut behind me, sending a gust of wind around my ankles as it did. George Fan, behind the hostess stand, gestured vaguely toward an empty booth in the barest demonstration of hospitality humanly possible. "You're back," she said tonelessly.

Parker gave her a quizzical look, and I offered a noncommittal shrug. "After you," he said to me, sweeping his hands out in a faux-chivalrous wave.

I stepped in front of him and led the way, refusing to allow myself to dwell on the fact that leaving him trailing behind me, beyond even the scope of my peripheral vision, made me suddenly uneasy, like someone had just tied a blindfold around my head.

Or bound my hands and ankles with twine, I realized. Kicked the footstool out from under me. Left me to swing, alone, from the gnarled arm of a crooked tree branch.

"Hey," Parker said, startling me again, but less aggressively this time. He passed a plastic-covered menu across the table to me. "You're looking so serious. What's on your mind?"

Hanged men. Ghosts. Curses. And someone—maybe you?— following me down dark alleyways, late at night.

His expression, though! So sincere. The tilt of his eyebrow, the concern on his face. *Please, please don't be a weirdo or stalker or some other kind of creep.* He was right—we were already in semideep, what with it being date-o'-clock, and if my runaway imagination had managed to pique my suspicions about Parker? I could only hope it would run back in the opposite direction soon enough.

"I'm starving," I said, taking the menu and flipping it open, avoiding the deeper question he'd been trying to ask. "Let's eat."

CHAPTER TWELVE

Wednesday

Caroline had been a little annoyed when I'd suggested that I was going to talk to Stephenson about her alibi. But that was fine by me. I was certainly no stranger to making a few enemies in service of a case. And now, with the lingering suspicion that someone had been following me, I wasn't worried about making things any worse with Caroline than they already were. And with my own mind cooking up some seriously disturbing images, I was even less inclined to care. I just wanted this case solved.

He kept "office hours" during lunch, which I guess was bad news for anyone who was struggling in English and yet still also wanting to eat. But then again, he generally made himself more available to students than a lot of other teachers, so maybe it was hard to give him too much flack for certain choices.

I found him in his classroom, surreptitiously wolfing down

a sandwich even though technically we weren't supposed to have food outside of the cafeteria. *Hmm. Not above flouting the rules. Duly noted.* Did that entitle him to more flack? Or less?

I mean, it was a truly minor infraction, but still. Right now, it was all about keeping an eye on rebellions, no matter how seemingly tiny or innocuous.

"Nancy Drew," he said with surprise in his voice as I rapped softly on the open door. He hurriedly stuffed his sandwich into a brown paper bag, which he tossed into a desk drawer, all within the blink of an eye. "What can I do for you?" He frowned, confused. "You got an A on that last essay, so I'm thinking it's not homework help." He folded his hands on his desk. "Please tell me you're not here to pick my brain about things you're not supposed to know about in the first place."

"Um, well . . . the good news is, I'm good on Henry James for right now," I said, though in truth I wouldn't have minded something a little less conventional on our curriculum. (Feminist fiction was an elective available for seniors, and I seriously couldn't wait.) "The less-good news . . . Well, actually, I kind of hope you don't mind, but I had some questions for you about Caroline Mark."

He raised an eyebrow at me, but his expression was unreadable. "Nancy," he started, using the tone that generally told me an adult was about to offer me some low-level scolding. (Sadly, it isn't too uncommon when you're known for being a low-level snoop.) "You know it's not appropriate for me to talk to you about another student if it doesn't directly concern you. Under any circumstances."

I sighed, settling into a front-row desk facing him, shaking my hair out of my face so I could look at him directly. "On the one hand: Yes, of course, I know that. And I understand. I'm not surprised that would be your response."

"I'm really looking forward to the 'but,' here," he said wryly.

"But . . ." I gave him a small, hopeful smile. "I actually spoke to Caroline about this already. She specifically sent me to you. So . . . maybe just the *one* circumstance, in this case?"

He took a deep breath and folded his arms on the desk. "This still smacks of unprofessionalism," he said, "but I suppose if you've already talked to her, there's no real harm in this conversation. I may as well hear you out."

It wasn't a resounding "yes." But it was good enough to spur me on. "Yesterday," I said, "in the morning. When Daisy Dewitt's locker was found vandalized." I didn't have to clarify further. It was a small enough school and a big enough shock; anyone who hadn't actually seen it with their own two eyes had heard about it by now.

Mr. Stephenson made a sympathetic noise. "Yes, I heard."

Two eyes: *check.*

"Awful. But what does that have to do with Caroline?"

"Mr. Stephenson," I said carefully, "the same way we all either saw or heard about Daisy's locker . . . *everyone* in school knows about how Caroline completely freaked out when she didn't get cast in the reenactment."

"True enough," he said. He scratched his chin. I couldn't help but think it looked like the gesture of someone who was stalling for time.

"In fact, *you* were the one who came out to comfort her on the quad—correct?" It was a rhetorical question. I remembered it vividly. That kind of demonstration was hard to forget.

Mr. Stephenson knew as much too. "Now, Nancy. If you're asking that question, I'm certain that you know that I was."

I shrugged. "Fine. Never mind. The reason I'm here is because, based on her reaction to the casting, Caroline is the student with the most obvious motive for trashing Daisy's locker."

"That feels like a stretch," he replied. "Even if she were unduly upset about the casting—and I can't say that I'd definitely categorize her reaction as such—"

I shot him a look, which he pointedly ignored.

"Even if she were *unduly* upset," he went on, emphasizing the word, "I don't see why that should translate to terrorizing Daisy in particular. I've never seen any specific animosity between those two. Again—not that I should really be discussing any of this with you."

"No specific animosity, per se," I agreed. "But Caroline was disappointed, whatever DEFCON level you personally feel comfortable assigning it. And Daisy's a legacy who got cast in a lead role. Maybe this was about Daisy . . . but maybe—and in my opinion, more likely—this was about the reenactment in general, and Daisy just happened to make for a very shiny target."

"I can't sign off on that theory, Nancy. I'm certain you know that, too."

He wasn't going to budge on this, and it wasn't super

surprising. This had essentially become a standoff. But I didn't actually need his sign-off on my theory. Only his confirmation that Caroline had been where she said she was yesterday.

"Okay. Well, then *you* know that, of course, I questioned Caroline about the vandalism."

"It's definitely not the most shocking thing I've heard all day," he said. "Not that I spend much time speculating about my students and their motives."

It's so cute when teachers try to get all clever on you.

"She said she was with you."

A good detective knows the signs of gifted liar: tiny micro-expressions and tells that might be lost on other, more trusting people. A good liar might use excessive superlatives when they talk to you; everything is "amazing" or "brilliant" instead of just plain "good." A liar might hesitate before telling you "no"; shifting in their seat, coughing, taking a breath before or after answering . . . all signs of a lie in process. A liar, under questioning, might speak more quickly than usual. He or she might refuse to look you in the eye.

Mr. Stephenson did none of those things. Mind you, I hadn't asked him a question as such, but it was more than implicit in my comment. He didn't fidget, or clear his throat, or fiddle with his clothes, or lob a question back in my direction. If anything, he seemed to get even *more* relaxed in that tiny millisecond of a moment while I waited, silent, giving him the space to compose a response.

"She was," he said simply.

I nodded, remaining quiet. If a good liar knows not to offer more details than what's being specifically asked for, then a good investigator has some tricks of her own up her sleeve too. And she knows to give the suspect space—and silence—to fill on their own, in their own time, potentially incriminating themselves.

"She's head of the Drama Club," he went on, completely unfazed to my eye. "We meet just the two of us every Tuesday morning for a check-in, since Tuesday after school is when Drama Club meets."

"Always in the morning?"

"Usually. It's easier to get it out of the way first thing, touching base. So that we're caught up before everyone else gets together."

Touching base. Okay. Plausible enough.

But "plausible" didn't always mean "true." Not to mention, if she was so high up in the Drama Club, it was all the more reason that she'd be outraged at not being cast in the reenactment.

"You were . . . in here?"

He shook his head. "The drama office."

Not an official *office* so much as a closet that had been repurposed as home base for productions. It was windowless and dusty and overrun with ancient costumes and yellowing sides from scripts that had accumulated throughout the years. It made total sense that as Drama Club president and Drama Club advisor they'd meet there.

It also made Caroline's alibi unprovable beyond Stephenson's confirmation.

Everything came down to whether or not I wanted to believe him.

Fact: I didn't have much reason not to, other than the nagging, ugly issue of Caroline being the only real suspect in the curse-related stuff, simply by virtue of having a convincing motive when no one else did.

Fact: If Stephenson was a liar, he was a convincing one.

Fact: *If* he was lying for Caroline—and I didn't particularly get the impression that he was—what was *his* motive?

I sighed. There wasn't one. Nothing obvious that I could see right now, anyway. If the worst thing he'd done was console a disappointed student who was in the throes of a very public meltdown, it didn't exactly scream "character flaw" to me.

He looked at me. "Have I satisfied your curiosity?" Then he wrinkled his brow. "Is there a world in which that would even be possible?"

I had to laugh. "Probably not. But yes. Thank you." I said it as sincerely as I could. "I appreciate your taking the time." I stood up.

"Nancy," he said, giving me pause. "While I think it's commendable that you're looking after your friend, I urge you not to jump to conclusions. Caroline is a . . . passionate student with a lot of energy. But she's got a good heart. I don't believe she'd ever lash out at a fellow student the way you're suggesting."

I shrugged. "I hope you're right, Mr. Stephenson," I said. "I've never had any problems with Caroline, myself. But I have learned a few times over now—the hard way, always—that people can sometimes surprise you. And not in a good way."

And what did it say that her alibi was working so hard to throw me off her trail? Was it possible that was actually more incriminating than if he weren't?

"So cynical." He looked slightly concerned.

"Not cynical," I corrected him, feeling my phone buzz in my pocket. "Just pragmatic. And I've gotta say, for the most part, it's worked out for me." I pulled out my phone and glanced at the message that had just come in. From Daisy, a group text to Lena and me. **Newspaper office. NOW. 911.**

Speaking of surprises, probably not of the good variety.

"Thanks. Again." I barely glanced at Stephenson now, as I shoved my notebook into my bag and gathered myself up. "I have to run."

"Take care, Nancy," he called as I raced from the room. But I didn't have time to reply.

Daisy wasn't one to use a "911" lightly. Another light fixture could have full-on exploded, and I wouldn't have stopped to take the stairs fewer than two by two. I think nothing short of nuclear fallout would have kept me from scrambling into the newspaper room, so that by the time I burst into the space, heart hammering, I was so out of breath that it took me a beat longer than normal to figure out what I was looking at.

When the image did resolve, though, it was a killer.

"What the hell?" I stammered, brushing my hair out of my eyes to step back and fully take in the scene. "What is this? *Who did it?*"

The classroom was absolutely *trashed*. Desks and chairs over-turned, angry spray paint dripping down walls, trash bins emp-tied over the teacher's desk at the front of the room. Someone had egged the whiteboard, bright, greasy yolks still running in clumpy streaks down the wall in places where they hadn't quite dried yet.

"What does that . . . say?" It was Lena, who'd sidled up beside me while I was still gaping, trying to process the chaotic scene.

I turned to see where she was pointing—the back wall of the room. The bulletin board that hung there had been stripped in angry, jagged slashes, ribbons of colorful paper now strewn across the floor. Over the now-blank canvas were words, bright red—the official color of this Naming Day curse, or so it was starting to seem.

LAST WARNING.

The bird.

Daisy's locker.

The message on my windshield.

Now this.

"What the hell does it mean?" I said, almost as much to myself as anyone else. Nothing good, that much I was sure of.

Daisy looked at us, helpless tears welling in her eyes. "I don't know who did this. Or why. It was . . . it was like this when I came by. I just . . . I had to pick something up. . . ." She trailed off, wordless, still in shock.

"You don't need to tell us why *you* were in here," I said gruffly. "Obviously, we trust you. But—something very, very messed up is happening here, Daisy. Someone is clearly targeting you. We can't just pretend these incidents are random or unconnected."

"Even if they were, each one on their own would be seriously bad news," Lena added.

"Well, yes," I agreed. "But there's no way we *still* think we can take them on their own . . . is there?" I glanced at both of my friends cautiously. I knew Daisy had been clinging to hope, long past a rational person's point of no return. But this was . . . something new. Un-ignorable. This told me just how borderline irresponsible I'd been in giving her the little bit of latitude that I already had.

I hesitated. I ignored my gut.

"Now my friends may be in danger." I didn't even realize I'd spoken out loud until I looked up to see both Lena and Daisy, closer now, real fear on both of their faces, a tear running down Daisy's cheek.

"You agree, right? You're on the same page with me?" I looked at Daisy, hesitant. Lena glanced my way and nodded, then put a hand on Daisy's shoulder.

Daisy blinked, wiping at her face. "Of course, Nancy. *Of course* I agree. I'm just . . . I'm embarrassed that it even took me this long. I should've been on board from the second the bird hit that window. I shouldn't have asked you to sit on it."

"You don't need to be embarrassed," Lena said, her voice

gentler than usual, reassuring. "We get that the festival was a big thing for you."

She sniffled. "Sure, yeah. A big thing. I get to star in the Naming Day reenactment at long last. How pathetically small-town-girl can you get?"

"It's not pathetic," I said, trying to match Lena's soothing tone with my own.

"It is a little," she insisted, trying to lighten the moment ever-so-slightly, for which I was grateful.

Lena laughed and nodded, holding two fingers up in that *kinda* sort of gesture. "Little bit," she admitted. "But we forgive you. Your small-town charm and whimsy are two of our favorite things about you, after all."

"Totally forgiven," I said before turning serious. "With one major caveat: that you're on board with me going all in on investigating this. *And* finally getting some authorities involved. This is two incidents of nasty vandalism—and if that whiteboard is permanently damaged, the school board is going to be *pissed*—and that's before you even bring in the whole thing with the, um, *threatening note tied to a dead bird.*"

"Super on board. Completely and totally. Like, I'm actually driving the bus. Except not literally, because I don't have a commercial license."

"I like where you're going with this metaphor," Lena said. "But please know, we'd never put you in charge of driving a bus. Just the Mini is more than enough responsibility for you."

"Mean," Daisy retorted, clearly not bothered—and not arguing, either.

"Ladies, I don't mean to break up this slumber party moment," a voice said, startling us all so we collectively jumped, "but I think we've officially gone beyond the point of sassy wordplay and into clear-and-present-danger-ville."

It was Theo, looming in the doorway, slouched just so and surveying the damaged room. His dark hair flopped over his eye, and he brushed it back from his forehead with a defiant tilt of his chin, looking at me with an implied challenge in his eye.

"Actually, fanboy, your timing is excellent," Lena said. "Because we are all in agreement: It's time to break out the big guns."

"Metaphorical guns; I *really* don't believe in violence," I said.

Theo waved his hand. He looked legitimately impatient. "More cutesy wordplay, girls. You don't seem to *get* it."

I rolled my eyes. "We do, though. The classroom was trashed. Next, it could be us." If I sounded flippant, I felt anything but. "We're on it. We're going straight to the principal to bring her into this. We're going to tell her everything. *Everything*," I added, with emphasis. "Including the raven."

"Forget the principal," Theo said.

Daisy looked confused. "But you just said—"

"Forget the principal, because she already knows. Well, she knows about some of it."

"You talked to her?" I asked, surprised. Also a little bit

irritated—this was *my* investigation, even if it was undercover.

"I had to. I mean, at least broad strokes. I'm sure there are plenty of details for you to fill in."

"Which broad strokes?" Casual, cavalier Theo going to the principal? *Before* he'd seen the trashed office?

He waved me off. "The good news is that unlike you three, *she* is actually truly on it. In that she's notified the chief, who's on his way to the school to investigate. There might even be an emergency assembly." But he didn't sound as cynically thrilled at those words as I might have expected. For once, Theo seemed truly distressed.

He looked at me. "She called your parents, too. Lawyer, social worker . . . seemed to think they'd be good types to have on hand in this kind of crisis."

My parents were coming? They were already in on this?

I glanced at Daisy and could see she was doing the same calculations I was. Her face was white.

"It's officially a crisis?" I asked, knowing the answer already, as I took in the blaring red graffiti on the whiteboard. "Did you even know about this room? Did you know it had been trashed?" My head was spinning.

He shook his head. "That's what I'm getting to. It's so much worse than you even know. Like, this"—he gestured at the ruined space of the classroom—"is not even the tip of the iceberg."

"*First this, then one of us,*" I said, my voice hoarse.

"That's what I've been trying to tell you. You're still one step behind, Nancy," Theo said.

Oh, no. I swallowed. "Who? What happened?"

His face crumpled in a way that made my stomach clench too. "No one knows what happened. That's why the police chief's on his way. We need to find her."

"Find who?" Daisy asked, desperate. *"Who's lost?"*

"It's Melanie," Theo said grimly. "She's gone."

PART TWO

THE VANISHING

Some say the town was founded in exchange for a sacrifice, for sacred blood. Only a very few—those who have lived in the town long enough to see through the cracks in the quaint veneer—think the history of Horseshoe Bay's very discovery is a testament to the poison at the root of our town's foundation. There are stories of incidents, of tragic events unfolding around Naming Days past.

The believers—they are the wise, while the foolhardy dismiss these as mere ghost stories, campfire tales, meant for sharing in the witching hour.

When the patriarch of one of Horseshoe Bay's oldest families was found drowned in his own bathtub? When the toxicology report showed high levels of muscle relaxants in his system? Those foolish people were quick to insist that his wife had slipped him the deadly medicine with his after-dinner brandy.

And the believers speculated, but one wanted to call it a curse.

Me? I called it karma.

CHAPTER THIRTEEN

Y ou mean to tell me there have actually been two incidents related to the reenactment and this so-called curse," Principal Wagner asked, sounding worried, stunned, and furious in equal measure. It really was something, to successfully squish so many different emotions into one single question—even a question as loaded as this one.

Principal Wagner, I can so relate.

I had at least as many big-time feelings competing for the number one slot too. The coincidence of hearing Glynnis's story just the night before and Melanie's disappearance did not elude me.

Principal Wagner's office was an inauspicious place to find oneself under the best of circumstances, and these circumstances definitely didn't qualify as "best." Or even, like, semigood. And yet here I was, stuffed into one of several stiff, uncomfortable office chairs arranged in a broad semicircle facing the principal's desk. I was flanked by Theo, Daisy, and Lena on one side, with my father, mother, and Chief McGinnis on the other. My friends, for their part, all looked varying degrees of worried, where the adults in the room were distinctly more furious. Safe to say, emotions were running high. Melanie's parents had been notified, and they were down at the police station.

"I knew about Ms. Dewitt's locker," Principal Wagner said. "Now there's this new . . . *development*." Her lip curled around the word, almost like an involuntary sneer.

"That's an awfully sanguine word for it," my father said. I knew his tone all too well—patient, measured, even. Someone who didn't know him the way I did might even think he was being friendly.

He wasn't. I could see from the way his eyes darted incessantly across the room, lighting on every surface before taking off again. He was taking it all in, evaluating. Principal Wagner had wanted a lawyer on hand? Well, here was Carson Drew, in full-tilt lawyer mode.

Principal Wagner cleared her throat. "Your response is understandable, Mr. Drew," she said. "And I've already spoken with Melanie's parents extensively. I'm only reluctant to name it as anything more ominous until given no choice. Right now, we just want to hear any additional information or details you might have." She glanced from my father back to me, her expression inscrutable.

Fair enough. But Dad's right: that was still a weirdly blasé way to put it.

Then again, Principal Wagner's bedside manner had always been a little bit lacking. Maybe it was too many years of dealing with high-strung parents and students who veered between intense type-A archetypes and total burnouts. I had to imagine it would take its toll.

"So," she said, her voice cutting through the tension in the room like glass, "Melanie was discovered missing today, and *you three*"—she looked at Daisy, Lena, and me—"discovered vandalism in the newspaper office."

"Meanwhile," Chief McGinnis cut in, "Daisy's locker was also found similarly vandalized yesterday morning, is that correct?"

Daisy nodded quietly. I leaned out of my seat to give her knee a squeeze.

My father and mother shot me a look almost in unison, as though it was something they'd practiced at home, or in the car together on their way over. *How you could you not have told us?*

I'm a teenage girl; I'm supposed to have some *secrets, aren't I?*

"Can I ask, Principal," McGinnis went on, his own tone taking on a condescending, almost menacing edge of its own now, "just how you know for a fact that the Forest girl is missing?" He was prickly, McGinnis, and suspicious by nature, which is, generally speaking, a good quality in a law enforcement official.

Generally speaking. Meaning, sometimes in theory more than in practice. I'd run up against his spikier sides on my own a few times, during different investigations. Even though he definitely meant well and was just trying to get the job done, sometimes it felt as though he and I were always working at cross-purposes. I preferred to think that was unintentional, a paranoid interpretation of things on my end.

"She was supposed to meet me," Theo said, leaning forward in his seat. "In the drama office. And then she didn't show."

"What were *you* doing in the drama office?" I asked, on instinct. That was the last place I would ever expect to find him.

Principal Wagner sighed and held up a hand. "Ms. Drew, if you'll allow *me* to direct this conversation?"

I gave her as abashed a look as I could muster. "Of course."

"Thank you." She looked at Theo. "Now: What *were* you doing in the drama office?"

Hmm. I guess it's the slight variation on inflection that makes all the difference.

Theo's cheeks reddened. "I was supposed to meet Melanie. To interview her."

"*Interview* her?" I blurted. I couldn't help myself.

"*Ms. Drew,*" Principal Wagner said, slower and more emphatic this time. "What did I just say?"

"Sorry, sorry," I mumbled. "It's just . . ." I whipped my head to stare at Theo, incredulous. "*Interview her?* On Monday, you were all about how ridiculous it was that the *Masthead* was even *covering* Naming Day for the paper."

He shrugged defensively. "Yeah, I guess. But, you know—Melanie and I were friends. *Are* friends." He blushed even harder. "She's not gone or anything. I mean, like, *permanently.* Missing isn't the same as gone."

"I should hope not," Principal Wagner put in.

"We'll find her," Chief McGinnis said, confident. "But, yes, she was supposed to meet Theo, but apparently never showed up at the drama office, which Theo discovered when he arrived to interview her."

"Interview her . . ." Even Lena was having a hard time taking it in. She glanced at Principal Wagner and held up her hands—*sorry, sorry!*—with a helpless look on her face. Principal Wagner just shook her head like she couldn't believe our ongoing impudence.

"She thought it would be fun, said it might even open my mind to the whole thing. And she . . . uh, well, she thought it would be fun to score a little extra publicity for her own appearance in the show, too."

"But we didn't even *assign* you the article," I said, still processing. This was literally the last thing I would have expected from Theo.

"What can I say? I'm full of surprises."

"So, what are our leads? Where do we think she is?" I asked automatically.

"Ms. Drew." This time it was McGinnis, slowing my name to an indignant drawl. "Are you determined to interject yourself into my investigation?"

"No! Of course not. I just want to help."

I mean, yes, actually. I was definitely determined to interject myself into the investigation. But: flies, honey . . .

"Now you want to help," he said. "Meanwhile, when you had something that might have tipped us off, might have helped us

see this coming and protect Melanie, you chose to keep quiet."

"It wasn't like that," I protested. "Well, I mean, I guess it *was*, but you have to believe me, I was doing it—we were *all* doing it—because we honestly thought the thing with the raven was just a prank." But I *hadn't* thought that. I'd only gone along with it because I was putting my friend's wishes first. I regretted it, even more than I could have anticipated.

"It was my idea to keep quiet," Daisy jumped in, her voice wobbly. "I just brushed the whole thing off as a prank. Or I tried to. I mean, a *Naming Day curse*? It sounded . . . ridiculous."

"And you didn't think it was potentially more dangerous, after your locker was vandalized?" Principal Wagner asked.

"I did," Daisy said quietly. "I just didn't *want* to think that."

"Denial," Theo said. "Powerful."

"How nice that you had the luxury to make that decision," she said, her voice silky despite the jagged edges of her words. "Unfortunately, Melanie may not have had such a say in her own fate."

Ouch. Don't pull any punches, Principal. She was right, of course; my low-key, on-the-DL investigation-lite of the curse might have been the crucial difference between Melanie's still being here, or being gone.

It was a mistake, I thought. *Listening to Daisy, even for a day or two.* I'd never forgive myself if something serious had happened to Melanie. What if she was hurt—or worse?

Don't think about that, I told myself.

I vowed to myself: Going forward, I wasn't going to hold back. *And* I'd follow my gut in full force—wherever it led.

"You're going to look at Caroline Mark, right?" That was Theo, his face open. "Question her?"

"Based on what you're telling me now, I have to say, she's pretty high on the list of suspects. She certainly sounds like one of the few students who's demonstrated a real motive." Chief McGinnis looked stern.

Wait, no. "But—" I protested. "She may have a motive, but she also has an alibi. She told me she was with Mr. Stephenson, and he confirmed that when I spoke with him."

"And I appreciate that input, Ms. Drew," the chief said, looking decidedly unappreciative. "And yet, I think I'll still pay Caroline a little visit, have a chat. That is, if you don't mind me taking my own approach to my own investigation."

"Of course not, sir," I said, my face feeling hot. But I did mind him *bungling* his own investigation. "It's just that, well— even if you put the Stephenson alibi aside—"

"And you'll be the first to know if I do," he said. "I hope that's okay?"

"No need to be so sarcastic," my father cut in, holding up a hand.

"Even if you did that," I went on, as smoothly as I could manage, "there's no way *Caroline Mark* could have, um, *kidnapped Melanie.* I mean, she's just a high school girl."

"Well, that's an interesting argument, *Nancy,* coming from a high school student who's essentially insisting that I take her seriously as a detective right now, wouldn't you say?" he replied, without missing a beat.

152 ~ MICOL OSTOW

I pressed my lips together tightly, looking away and refusing to give him the satisfaction of a response. Even still, I could feel my mother's eyes on my turned back, offering a sympathetic glance.

"If there are other leads—ones that you care to share with me, that is," he went on, "I can assure you we'll be investigating those as well."

"I won't be holding back," I said solemnly. I was still embarrassed for having possibly helped Melanie come to harm, even as I resented McGinnis for obviously trying to rub it in and make me feel as bad as he possibly could. Worried, too.

"We're glad to hear it," Principal Wagner said, as prim as ever.

"Did you need anything more from us?" my father asked. He looked tense, ready to bolt from his seat. It wasn't about the case, I knew. He just wasn't crazy about Principal Wagner and her, uh, *severe* personality, as he liked to put it.

My mother put a steadying hand on his knee. "I know Carson will be available if you have further questions." Of the two of them, she was the one who could smooth over just about any social interaction, no matter how awkward.

And this one is getting nice and awkward.

"Of course," he said. "And the bottom line is that the school isn't liable for Melanie's disappearance."

"Well, that depends on what sort of evidence our investigation turns up," McGinnis added.

My father tilted his head, reluctantly considering it. "Sure. There are always exceptions to rules, of course."

NANCY DREW: THE CURSE ~ 153

"And *of course*," Lena chimed in, eyes flashing, "*liability* is what we're all thinking about right now, after a girl has disappeared from our campus."

"You can climb down off of your soapbox, Ms. Barrow," Principal Wagner said. "We are just as concerned about Ms. Forest as you are."

"Yeah, it definitely sounds that way," Lena said, pushing it. I gave a not-so-delicate throat clearing to suggest that she take it down a notch or two, and she folded her arms over her chest in a huff.

"But in the meantime, if I can be of any assistance to the chief's department, please do let me know," my father went on. "*That* was the crux of what I was getting at just now."

Lena gave another little snuffling sound, pulling her arms tighter against herself, but she managed not to actually say anything this time, at least.

"And, if I may," my mother said, her eyes wide and her face open, "I'm happy to make time to meet with the school counselor to go over some pointers for crisis counseling. Or I can set up office hours of my own here to see students. Or lead an assembly . . . whatever you think is best. I'm sure the students will have questions and feelings to process."

I looked at my mother, flooded with love. Where I saw puzzles to solve, she saw people to help. It was amazing.

"Thank you, Ms. Drew," Principal Wagner said, offering her first sincere smile since this meeting had begun. My mother had that effect on people. It was a quality that seemed to have

154 of MICOL OSTOW

"Great," said the chief, rising. "If we're through here for now, I'm going to try to catch Caroline Mark. Does anyone know where she'd be right now?"

"You can check with the office assistant out front; she keeps the class schedules and student files," Principal Wagner said.

"She has a study period," Theo cut in. "But, uh, she's not on campus, I don't think. She mentioned that she was taking her car into the shop. We can check the lot to see if it's still there."

"What's wrong with her car?" Chief McGinnis asked, at the same time as the question scrolled across the inside of my own head.

Theo shrugged. "I don't have details. She mentioned it in homeroom, is all. Something about the headlights being funky. Or one headlight?"

My breath caught in my throat. *Headlights.*

The twin beams, one flickering, darkening briefly.

Me, alone on the road back from Stone Ridge.

Pale, grime-streaked ankles in my rearview mirror, bound by twine.

It had felt, that night, like someone was *watching* me. And then there was that message on the windshield—there one minute, gone the next. A figment of my imagination? Or someone messing with me?

I opened my mouth to say something about it. *Go with your gut*, the echo refrained.

But my gut, this time, was telling me to *stay* on the DL, just a little while longer. Yes, Melanie was missing, and yes, the stakes were unignorable. But I didn't believe that *Caroline Mark* had planned and executed an abduction any more than I believed that I'd seen the ghost of a hanged man in my rearview mirror.

My gut was telling me to let Chief McGinnis follow whatever lead he was sniffing after. Because that gave me more time to do a little digging of my own. If Caroline Mark wasn't the primary suspect, then who was? And was the flickering headlight—or the memory of a car tailing me the other night—purely a figment of my imagination, or worse?

I didn't even know what the "worse" would be in this situation. I didn't want to think too hard about it. The situation had already spun out of control. And I'd broken my own oath to be totally open with Principal Wagner and the chief . . . before I'd even left this office.

What can I say? I'm really *not the best at taking orders.*

My parents and I were leaving the principal's office when Daisy's mother arrived.

"What are you doing here?" Daisy asked, her face going pale at the sight of her mother.

Her mother looked gaunt, drawn, smaller than I remembered her. She wore a long wool skirt—unseasonably long; it looked like it would be uncomfortable in this early spring weather— with a simple white blouse and a scarf printed with a bright red emblem of a bird. I recalled Daisy once mentioning that robin redbreasts were her mother's favorite, which was maybe the only personal detail I'd ever heard about Mrs. Dewitt.

"The principal asked me to come talk to her about this . . . *curse* business," she said, her voice low. Daisy shot me a look.

"Mrs. Dewitt," I gushed, feeling awkward and desperately wanting to take some heat off of Daisy. "The principal is on top of whatever's going on. You don't need to worry."

She gave me a small, icy smile. "So on top of it that no one can say exactly what *is* going on, then?"

Touché.

"Get to class, Daisy," her mother said to her ominously. "I'll find you when I'm done."

Daisy cast me another glance, but there was nothing I could do.

Parker: Did I see you coming out of the main office with your parents and Chief McG?

Nancy: *blushes* Busted.

Parker: Everything all right?

Nancy: With me? Yes.

Nancy: Less so with Melanie Forest. From the newspaper.

Parker: Of course, I know Melanie. And yeah, I heard.

Nancy: Well, news like that travels fast.

Parker: So what did the chief want with you?

Parker: Wait, does he think this is connected to Daisy's locker? And the thing with the raven?

Nancy: It's hard not to think they might be linked. Also the newspaper office getting trashed.

Parker: Wait—that one, I hadn't heard about yet.

Nancy: In that case, let me be the bearer of bad news. . . .

Parker: Lunch on the quad? We can talk for real.

Nancy: Assuming we're not all called into a crisis counseling assembly, you're totally on.

Parker: Just one more thing for you to fill me in on.

Parker: Bad news aside, looking forward.

Nancy: Me too. See you at lunch.

CHAPTER FOURTEEN

If the tension had been thick in Principal Wagner's office that afternoon, dinner with my parents was thicker than the pea-soup-style fog that rolls over the surface of the bay. After an excruciatingly silent salad course where I could hear every last crunch of kale reverberating in my ears, I had to say something.

"Okay, guys, just let me have it," I begged. "Say whatever you need to say. This 'polite, repressed silence stretched over a simmering rage' thing is a little bit stressful, I'm not gonna lie."

My father took a deep breath and gripped at his fork and his knife in either hand, clanking them loudly against the edges of his plate.

As usual, it was my mother who stepped in, swift and graceful, setting her own fork down and taking a sip of water before taking the plunge. "There's no 'simmering rage,' sweetie," she started. "Although I *will* give you bonus points for teenage angst set to eleven."

"Teenage angst?" I raised an eyebrow at that. "Let me be the first to point out that *you're* the ones giving *me* the silent treatment."

"We're just worried about you," my mother said. "You know we always try to be supportive of your investigations—much more than lots of parents."

Fair.

"But try to see it from our point of view, sweetie. Someone sent a threatening note to you at the school paper, and you didn't think to mention it to us?"

"Someone sent *a* threatening note to *someone* at the school. We have no way of knowing that it was specifically sent to the newspaper office. And yes, it was creepy—good job on the originality and terror factor, whoever came up with the plan in the first place—but as *many* people on the newspaper staff pointed out, Keene High is the very same school where our soccer rivals' underwear were found hanging from a flagpole the night before the final game of the season. Pranks are not taken lightly here. This wouldn't have been the wildest prank we'd ever seen here."

"This 'prank' was calculated," my father said, his voice low and tight.

Point: Dad. The bird thing was not *not* a concern. "I'm . . . looking into it," I said weakly. I didn't dare mention my nightmare; it would definitely set them off—Mom especially—into a flurry of armchair analysis—words like "trauma" and "repressed memories" rushing across the table in a fit of concern.

"That's just the point, Nancy," my father finally said, his voice rising. "Are you *trying* to be obtuse here? Because that's exactly what we're upset about. You 'looking into it.'"

I stared at him. "You can't honestly expect me to leave this alone. You think someone's targeting my friends, possibly me, and you want me to just sit around doing nothing?"

"I expect you to let Chief McGinnis do his job," Dad said. "Which, by the way, he *can't* do effectively if you and your friends that you're so worried about are all keeping secrets and withholding information."

"Dad, he has *one* lead." I looked at them both, one after the other, begging them with my eyes to hear me, to take me seriously. "You know as well as I do that the chances that Caroline Mark had anything to do with Melanie's disappearance are slim to none. They should be looking at Melanie's family, old boyfriends . . ." My father *knew* these things. It was Police Work 101. Mom's best friend, Karen, was a detective with the force, for Pete's sake. Speaking of being deliberately obtuse.

"Nancy, we know you're skilled at investigative reporting," my mother started.

"Mom," I said, "it's more than just reporting. Whether you want to admit it or not."

She sighed and closed her eyes, like I was a headache located right at the bridge of her nose. Or, if I wasn't *the* headache, I was definitely the cause of one. "Fine. True. You're a talented investigator, and it's a quality we treasure in you."

"Funny." I laughed, short and bitter. "I'm not feeling so *treasured* right now."

"Well, that's because it's complicated. Because, talented or not, you are still a teenager, and you're still *our child*. You'll forgive us for prioritizing your own safety above all else. Don't you get that, Nancy?" Her voice cracked on my name, and my own resolve along with it.

Now it was my turn to sigh. "I do," I admitted. "Of course I do." My parents had always supported me—even after I solved my first case, which the chief hadn't been too happy about. Catching a child molester? Good. Catching a child molester based on intel an elementary school girl had come up with when your own squad had turned up zilch? Not as good. At least, not for his ego.

But still, my parents had stuck by me.

They had to get it, though—that sometimes coming forward right away wasn't the best course of action. That grown-ups, authorities—even the good guys, the ones we trusted to keep us safe and to protect us—could make mistakes, could be blinded to certain clues and details.

I knew, in that moment: *Of course* they got it. But "getting it" still paled in comparison to their worry for me.

I glanced across the table to Mom again, processing the icy spike of fear that jabbed my ribs as she rubbed at her temples, like this conversation—like *I*—was causing her actual, physical pain.

I got it. Just like they did. I got it too.

There were no bad guys here. Well, other than the obvious ones, like whoever was "pranking" our school, and whoever was responsible for Melanie's disappearance. But my parents weren't trying to give me grief. Just like I wasn't trying to make trouble for them, or cause them concern.

We were all doing the best we could.

Unfortunately for me, in this case, that meant making things a little bit worse—maybe more than a little bit—before they could get any better.

"I hear what you're saying," I said slowly. I set my fork down. "And I promise to be more careful. *And* more honest," I added, before my father could cut in. "But . . ." Here, I knew, I had to tread lightly. "I do have a question."

My father sighed, but at last, there was a slight sparkle in his eye. "Of course you do. You wouldn't be our kid if you didn't."

I grinned, but it faded, as I anticipated what was coming next, what I was about to potentially unleash. "The note on the bird, Daisy's locker, the graffiti in the newsroom . . ."

The message etched on my windshield, in the frost.

"They all referenced a Naming Day curse."

My father rolled his eyes. "Horseshoe Bay does love its curses." He gave a patient smile in Mom's direction. "You know we don't buy into all that."

"No, I know. Totally." It was my constant refrain, after all. *Only what I can see with my own two eyes.*

But I *had* seen it. That was the thing. That was the part that was gnawing away at me, boring a hole in my belly, keeping me awake at night.

"It's just weird how all three of those things mentioned it. And yet, no one I know seems to have ever even heard of this curse."

"It's not *that* weird if it's all driven by the same person," my dad pointed out.

"Fair. Okay, but . . . so, like you said, Horseshoe Bay has so many random little quirky traditions, rituals, superstitions . . . Naming Day itself is just a small part. And the curse is like this little throwaway, nothing anyone ever makes a real thing about. So there are no details going around about what, exactly, the curse itself even is."

"I'm sure there never were any details in the first place," my father said, waving his hand dismissively. "Like you say, it was just another one of those random, quirky stories. Nobody says anything because there's nothing to say. Nothing to tell."

"Daisy's mom seemed to think otherwise," I pointed out. "She didn't even want Daisy to be in the reenactment."

My mother coughed delicately into her napkin. "Daisy's parents are . . ." She trailed off, uncertain. "Well, you know exactly how they are, sweetie. Eccentric. There's a reason we didn't let you stay at Daisy's house when you were little."

"The *reason* was that her parents didn't want people sleeping over. Because they're private," I said. "Right?" Suddenly, I wasn't so sure.

"You don't remember, do you?" my mother asked suddenly. "I just assumed, since you've got such a steel trap of a mind when it comes to most things . . ."

A fist clenched in my stomach. "Don't remember what?"

"It wasn't a big thing," my mother said. "You went to Daisy's once, when you were very little. A sleepover. When we picked you up in the morning, you were terrified."

"Something *scared* me?" That was a new one.

"Well, yes—we thought it was strange too. Or we never

would have let you go in the first place. You were fine, and the Dewitts couldn't tell us what had happened. Mostly, they seemed embarrassed, so since you were obviously okay, we didn't push it. But you never did tell us what had you so worked up.

"And the Dewitts never asked you back, which was fine with us. As far as we could tell, that was the beginning and the end of Daisy's slumber parties."

My mind reeled. I couldn't believe I had somehow blanked out on that entire experience. And more to the point: What could possibly have terrified me so badly at Daisy's?

And whatever it was, was it somehow still relevant today?

Suddenly, the calm of the dinner table was broken with the sound of my phone chiming in my pocket. My mother shot me a look.

I nodded—*I know*—but pulled my phone out and peeked at it under the table anyway. I looked at my mom. "I mean, there's a student missing," I said apologetically.

"Be quick," she said, but there was no real scold to her voice.

"It's Daisy," I said, rising from the table. "Excuse me for a minute?"

I stepped into the living room for a little privacy, without waiting for a reply.

Daisy: How's it going with the parentals?

Nancy: Touchy, in a word. No one's exactly thrilled with the new developments at school . . . or the fact that I kept clues to myself all this time.

Daisy: Yeah, still sorry about that.

Nancy: Forget it. I knew what I was doing. I can own my own choices.

Daisy: Well, thanks for that. But here's the thing: My parents are being weird. Like, weirder than usual.

Nancy: ?

Daisy: Remember when I told you they weren't so thrilled about me being in the reenactment?

Nancy: Yeah, that totally was weird.

Daisy: IKR? But it gets better. At dinner we were talking about Caroline, my mom having to come into school to talk to the chief and Principal Wagner.

Nancy: Yeah, that was pretty rough.

Daisy: Rough would have been a welcome improvement. But the thing was, they were so upset to hear that McGinnis is questioning Caroline, but that he still hasn't shut down all the Naming Day stuff. Like given all those threats and mentions of this mysterious curse. Apparently, they think it really should be stopped.

Nancy: I don't like it. Something doesn't add up.

Daisy: Nancy Drew, on the case.

Daisy: I'm not worried. I know we're in good hands.

Daisy: McGinnis is going to crack Caroline like a walnut, and this nightmare will be behind us.

Nancy: . . .

Daisy: That was a joke. Your hands are the good ones, of course. But I am happy that McGinnis is looking into Caroline.

That he seems to have a plan, I mean. One that doesn't involve putting a stop to Naming Day.

Nancy: Yet, anyway.

Daisy: Always so optimistic! I am choosing to be hopeful. I'm crossing my fingers that the Caroline lead pans out, and that we can all start to move forward and put this drama behind us. That Melanie's returned home safe, and Naming Day goes off without a hitch.

Nancy: . . .

Without another *hitch*, I'd been beginning to type. But I didn't have a chance to finish my message, because just then, the doorbell rang. **BBS**, I wrote quickly to Daisy.

"Nancy!" My mother called me from the front door. "You have a visitor."

A visitor? I wasn't expecting anyone. I smoothed my hair behind one ear and walked to the front hallway.

It was Parker, leaning in the doorway, giving me his adorably crooked smile. "I was just in the neighborhood."

I laughed. "Well, we do live in the same neighborhood," I pointed out.

"I know! It makes this whole *oh, I just dropped by* thing so much more convincing. It's awesome. And very convenient."

"Nancy," my mother said, "your gentleman caller was saying he wanted to take you to the Frosty Queen."

"I was," he said. "I was craving one of those M&M mixer things."

I peered at him. "It's a little cold for ice cream, but I'm game."

I looked back at my mother. "And please don't ever say 'gentleman caller' again."

"You can pick the activity this weekend, if you like," he said, holding his arm out for me to link mine through.

"Did we have plans for the weekend?"

"Well, I was hoping we could," he said.

"Ooh, Nancy, this one's a charmer," my mom said. I could tell from her expression that she liked Parker.

That was good, because I did too. He was sharp enough to keep up with me, and so far, he didn't seem weirded out by my girl-detective thing. I'd started to wonder if such a guy even existed.

"And yes, you're excused from dinner," she said, winking.

"Hang on just a second," I told him. "I'll grab my coat."

"A random ice cream run," I said. "Good instinct."

"I know. Admit it," he said, walking me to the shotgun side of his car and opening the door for me—*a charmer*, just like Mom had said; it was so true. "Now that I've mentioned it, you can't get the idea of ice cream mixed with M&M's out of your mind."

"I admit nothing," I said. Then I burst out laughing as he got into the car and revved the engine. "But you're totally right."

"I'm always right," he said. "You'll learn that about me soon enough. It's one of my best qualities."

"Funny," I said. "Around here, I'm kind of known for always being right too."

"That *is* funny," he replied. "I guess the two of us together will be basically unstoppable."

He was teasing, but his words still made me go all melty inside. Which was nice, because though the heat was on, the car was definitely still chilly.

He turned on the headlights.

My blood ran cold.

This time, it had nothing to do with the temperature in the car.

"Your . . . headlights . . . ," I stammered. "One of them's flickering."

"What? Oh, yeah." He ran his hand through his hair, distracted. "It's been doing that lately. Weird. I should take it in. Which mechanic do you recommend, neighbor?" he asked playfully.

"Um, J. Dodd's," I mumbled. "They're the best."

"I'm guessing in a town like Horseshoe Bay, they're also the *only*, right?" Parker rubbed his hands together, blowing on them. "Damn, Nancy . . . you may be right about ice cream being a bad idea tonight. I'm, like, chilled to the bone."

Me too. But for very different reasons.

"Nancy? Hey—are you okay?" Parker turned to me, concerned. He brushed a hand across my cheek. "You suddenly look like you've seen a ghost."

"What?" I hated to admit it, even with the slow crawl of dread across my skin, his hand on my face made me tingle. "Sorry, no. Just . . . spaced out there, for a minute."

"Well," he said, a grin spreading across his own perfect face. "Let's see what we can do to bring you back into the moment."

He leaned in and kissed me softly.

If I'd been cold a moment before? Now my whole body was on fire.

In that moment, I knew my parents could totally see us through the living room window—if they were looking, which wasn't typical of them, but then again, they *were* parents. I knew something strange—something dangerous—was still swirling out there, around us, somehow connected to Naming Day, curse or no.

And I knew that Parker's headlight was flickering, just like Caroline's had. Just like the car that followed me the other night.

Meaning, maybe I had another suspect to add to my list now.

I look like I've seen a ghost? Parker had no idea. He couldn't imagine what it was like to look into a mirror and see those pale, lifeless legs dangling in the glass. And right now, wrapped in his arms and taking in the warm scent of him with every breath?

Anything would have been preferable to what I actually saw in my mind when I shut my eyes.

Twin beams, bearing down on me, on a lonely deserted road.

Could it have been Parker?

I pulled him to me tighter now, willing the thought away. If only for the moment.

CHAPTER FIFTEEN

Thursday

More auspicious than Parker's car troubles the night before was the eager honk of Daisy's Mini from outside my house, bright and early the next morning.

Thank freaking God.

In the end, it turned out an icy-cold Flurry *was* exactly what the two of us needed last night, and it was definitely what *I* needed to dive straight into the sweet oblivion of a massive brain freeze. If I concentrated deeply enough, I could still feel the tiny sugar crystals and the crunch of the M&M shells on my tongue.

Not to mention the feel of Parker's hands running through my hair.

I hadn't been able to put the flickering headlight totally out of my mind on our date—I wouldn't have been myself, if I had. But I *was* able to put it in a box, somehow, tightly shut and neatly stored in some far-flung corner of my brain, just for a few hours. I thought of it as the filing cabinet of my subconscious, and what I *really* didn't want to dwell on right now was the fact that, directly adjacent to the WHAT'S THE DEAL WITH PARKER'S HEADLIGHTS? file, was one marked, ANOTHER SHADOWY NIGHTMARE, THIS TIME WITH THE NEWSROOM UP IN FLAMES, CONSUMED, AS A HANGED CORPSE SWAYS FROM A LIGHT FIXTURE IN THE MIDDLE OF THE ROOM.

Feathers cling to the tattered hem of her dress.

A discolored string of dainty pearls—the one she always wears— around her neck like a noose.

It's Daisy.

The hanged girl—it's Daisy.

I woke up from *that* stunner screaming, bathed in sweat, flailing, and grabbing desperately at my sheets. After a moment, though, as my eyes adjusted to the sunlight, I realized where I was—home—and, more important, that I was safe.

For now.

I sat in bed, gasping for breath, waiting for one or both of my parents to come racing in to see what I'd been screaming about, willing my heartbeat to slow to a normal pace and practicing at my "casual, nonchalant" response. But no one came, so instead, I took a steamy shower, longer than usual, luxuriating in the scalding water beating down on me like needles, needing the intensity of that sensation to scour away the lingering images from my dream. By the time I was dressed and downstairs, waiting on Daisy and Lena, the sun was out in full and it was easy to imagine that indeed, I *was* safe, here and now.

Mom and Dad were both in the kitchen, arguing amiably

over the newspaper, which they both still read in print, religiously, every morning over coffee, eggs, and toast. They were each wearing running clothes—sleek leggings and some high-tech top for Mom, old-school sweats and a fleece for Dad—and earbuds dangled around their necks.

Not earbuds. A ruined, crumbling string of pearls.

I took a deep breath, and when I looked again, they were just earbuds again.

You're losing it for real now. Or maybe I'd already *lost* it, past tense, and then what?

"You guys went . . . running," I managed. Here was that "casual, nonchalant" thing I'd been working on in the bedroom, and thank goodness for that.

It wasn't totally uncommon for either of them, the morning run, but it wasn't a regular thing. "You guys know date nights are supposed to be at *night*, right? And they're supposed to incorporate actual fun? Not *exercise*." I mock-shuddered.

"Ha ha," my mom said, tossing a balled-up napkin at me. "Maybe it's corny, jogging together—"

"Oh, it's *definitely* corny," I assured her. "At best."

"Don't tease a poor old woman." She laughed. "It's just that I've been feeling so stressed lately," she said.

"So naturally, a run at the crack of dawn was the only solution."

"More like a last resort. But I didn't make it up, I promise! I read an article that said that high-impact movement first thing in the morning can have a huge positive impact on energy levels and cognition," she insisted.

"That's why you've got to stop reading the news. It'll rot your brain," I joked. I looked at Dad. "You support this?" He was an athletic guy, very fit for a dad. (My friends sometimes allowed that he was cute, for a dad, which was totally intolerable information.) But a tandem run still felt very next-level.

"Your mom wanted to give it a try," he said, taking a long swig of his coffee. "Who am I to stand in her way?"

"Who, indeed?" At least they liked each other, which was more than I could say for lots of my friends' parents. Loved, even. That was never in question. I was lucky that way. We all were, our little family. I was relieved that there wasn't any lingering tension from our semi-argument the night before.

"You okay there, Nancy?" my dad asked, peering at me. "You've gone off into a little reverie." He snapped his fingers for emphasis.

I shook my head, realizing he was right. I blinked and was surprised to discover hot tears pricking at the corners of my eyes.

Settle down, Drew. A little gratitude was a good thing, sure, but there was no need to be having a Lifetime movie moment right here in the kitchen, out of the blue, coffee machine burbling away on the counter.

Still shaken up by that dream, I decided, and was pouring myself my own cup of coffee when, mercifully, Daisy's horn beeped outside.

"Do us a favor, Nancy," my mother said. "Promise you'll focus on school today, and not mysteries."

I didn't want to lie to them. "I'll do my best," I said. I kissed them each a quick good-bye and ran to meet my friends.

*   *   *

"I overslept," I said, breathless, as I shimmied into the back seat and brushed my hair from my shoulders. "Didn't even have time for a cup of coffee. Weird . . ." *Weird dreams*, I'd started to say, before realizing I didn't want to get into it just then.

"Well, good thing we're going *for coffee*," Lena drawled.

"Yeah, Nancy"—Daisy cast me a quick look via her rearview mirror—"you did agree to meet so we could hit Harbor Joe's before school, right? Like, that was the whole plan?"

"Of course."

The truth? I knew that we'd made plans to meet up this morning, and Harbor Joe's made the most sense—it was one of the only places open this early, anyway—but I'd been so distracted by that dream that the specifics of our text thread from the night before had gone straight out of my head. But I wasn't about to admit that.

"So spacey this morning!" Daisy said, practically trilling. She was grinning from ear to ear and fiddling with the presets on her radio, finally settling on some aggressively chipper pop station.

"I'm gonna get a cavity listening to this," Lena protested. "I mean, are you kidding me with it?"

"What?" Daisy shrugged. "I'm in a good mood. The chief is investigating Caroline, he's on the case, *and* he hasn't canceled Naming Day, which I know is what my parents were pushing for. It's all very win-win."

"I mean, not for Melanie," I pointed out. "But I hear you."

"Am I allowed to be excited about Naming Day *at the same*

time as I'm worried about Melanie?" Daisy asked. "Because I swear to you on my own role in the reenactment, I'm both."

"You're allowed," I said. "But given that someone is actually missing, maybe let's take it down twenty percent."

"Nancy's right. Just play it cool around people who aren't us," Lena warned. "If you seem too happy, *you'll* end up a suspect."

We all had to laugh at that. Daisy was the sweetest, friendliest, kindest girl in our grade, maybe in the whole school. The idea that she would be behind a kidnapping and sabotage was literally laughable.

"I'll be cool, I promise. If you guys agree to one tiny detour this morning."

"Where?" I asked, wary, but glancing out the window, I'd already guessed what she had in mind.

We were headed in the general direction of Harbor Joe's, but Daisy took a sharp left as we came to the intersection, veering in the opposite direction, to the immediate outskirts of town, just beyond the bay, where the fairgrounds lay. In the distance, the gray-green ocean glittered in the morning sun.

"They haven't started putting up the scaffolding for the reenactment," I told her. "I think that's supposed to start later this afternoon. There won't be anything to see yet."

"I know," she said, her shoulders hunching guiltily. "But I'm excited. I still want to take a peek. And it's kind of on the way, right?"

"In the sense of being exactly in the opposite direction at

the intersection, sure." Lena shrugged. "But as long as we get out of here with enough time to hit Harbor Joe's before first period, I'm cool."

"You *are* cool!" Daisy agreed, exuberant as ever. "We're *all* cool. The coolest."

"Daisy?" Lena was tentative, guarded.

"There will be plenty of time to get coffee!" Daisy said, feigning exasperation.

"No, there won't," I said flatly, seeing what Lena was looking at.

Coffee is officially off the morning agenda, I realized, my heart sinking.

"We've got to go straight to school to talk to Principal Wagner. And she's gonna have to loop McGinnis in," I finished.

Daisy didn't protest. The jocularity had drained from her face, now pale and clammy. Her eyes darted back and forth as she surveyed the scene:

The fairgrounds, typically a broad, grassy expanse. But today, patches had been burned dead-to-center in the lawn to reveal yet another dark, ominous warning. I shook my head, blinked. Looked again. It was still there.

Daisy swallowed. "You're seeing this, right? You're both seeing this?"

"We are," I said, as Lena nodded.

There, in the grass, each scorched letter at least three feet high and just as wide, was the ugly message:

TIME'S UP.

*　　*　　*

"Oh, good," I said weakly, as we pulled into the Keene High parking lot. "Chief McGinnis beat us here."

"Maybe *he* brought coffee," Lena quipped darkly.

As Daisy parked, the three of us took in the tableau: two police cars, thankfully parked and silent, in the emergency vehicle lane up along the front entrance to the school. A gaggle of concerned Keene teachers clustered along the sidewalk, bottlenecking into a staggered throng of parents up the front steps and through the open doors. Anxious chatter rose in a din.

I looked at Lena and Daisy. Neither of their parents were immediately visible in the group, but that didn't mean they weren't in there—you could have shoved a small dinosaur into the middle of that mob and it would have taken a while for even me to sniff it out. Wordlessly, we grabbed hands and moved down the pathway to the side entrance to the school.

"Now, do *you* want to be the one to tell the chief what we saw?" Lena asked, as we entered the building. "Because I dunno, Nancy—I feel like you kind of have a way with these authority figures."

Ha. "Yeah, a way of ticking everybody off."

"The good news is, he already seems *super* ticked," Daisy pointed out. She gestured.

We hadn't even made it halfway down the hall before we stumbled onto the scene. A row of lockers, one thrown open, the chief flanked by three other officers. (Horseshoe Bay was so small, it felt odd that we even *had* that many officers available to report to a crime scene, but I guess it never hurt to be prepared.)

One had a menacing-looking German shepherd at the end of a leash, standing alert, tail extended, at his heel.

"Whose locker is that?" Daisy asked. "And—just curious— what, exactly, do you think McGinnis is having those dogs sniff for?"

"I'm going to go out on a limb," Lena said, "and guess that the locker is Caroline Mark's."

It was hanging open now, and while Chief McGinnis's body was blocking our view of the contents, the two officers behind him who weren't handling the dog were carefully bagging items from it in large, meaty gloved hands.

One of those items? A can of red spray paint.

And in two other, smaller bags: what looked like a lipstick and a nail polish, respectively.

"Taking bets on what color you think that lipstick is," I murmured. *Bloodred, no doubt.* No bookie alive would take those odds.

"So she *was* the one who trashed my locker? And the newsroom?" Daisy said, forehead furrowed.

"Looks that way," I replied.

Which could mean: Someone out there wanted *it to look that way.*

Then again, she did have means and motive. She'd been on my own suspect list, after all. And Stephenson, her alibi, could have had reasons of his own for covering for her. I'd definitely seen stranger things in other investigations.

But still: my gut.

That curse. My dream. The visions in my rearview window.

Two people whose headlights were mysteriously malfunctioning on and off—one of whom I'd recently learned I very much liked to kiss.

Perhaps it *could* be that simple. Maybe Caroline was behind all the vandalism, and looking into planted evidence, etc., was just wandering too far down bizarre conspiracy-theory paths. *Maybe* I could get on board with that, tell my gut to calm down, at least for a beat or two, while we sorted this whole mess out.

But that still didn't account for Melanie.

I was processing, mulling the various threads over, as McGinnis cleared a path for himself and his officers through the gathered students and other rubberneckers. "Excuse me," he bellowed, loud enough that his words bounced off the tiled hallway wall. "Coming through. We need to get by. Thank you for cooperating."

But no one *was* cooperating, not really. Students craned their necks, and the various assistants from the front office hovered anxiously at a just-close-enough remove. (No one was fooled.) Principal Wagner stood in the midst of it all, hands on hips. Her expression was stern, her face stony. Behind McGinnis, another uniformed officer had an arm around the shoulder of one Caroline Mark. A courtesy, I guessed—kinder than leading her off in handcuffs, which theoretically felt like overkill. Until you remembered the carnage at Daisy's locker, the newsroom . . . and the missing student, who still hadn't been found.

I grabbed the shoulder of a passing student. "What time did McGinnis get here?" I demanded.

He shrugged, eyeing me warily. "Not sure. Not too long ago. Maybe just after the school doors opened."

Not helpful. Doors officially opened at seven for staff, and students who wanted to grab breakfast at the school—a small group, but it existed—could come in as early as seven thirty.

Did that give Caroline enough time to have burned the lawn at the fairgrounds? If she was responsible for the locker and the classroom, did that make her the most likely culprit for the warning sign in the grass, too? Or was that just what someone wanted us to think? Someone, for instance, who had Melanie stashed away somewhere, and wanted to be sure we were busy looking elsewhere instead of hunting them down?

I flashed back to the fairgrounds: the grass had been placid (albeit singed), not smoky. Which meant the burning had been done at least a few hours before we arrived. Time enough for the air to clear.

It could have been Caroline. She could have done it overnight.

But "could have" wasn't "did." There was more work to be done. And meanwhile, Melanie was still missing without a trace.

The clock was ticking.

Boldly, I stepped in front of McGinnis as he swaggered down the hall, a Pied Piper leading his own grim band in a short, tense trail behind him. He rolled his eyes when he registered me. "Of course. Nancy Drew. Just what my day was missing." He gestured at his team, everything they'd collected. "You'll be happy to know that after we got a warrant to search Caroline Mark's locker, we were able to gather enough evidence to question her about the recent spate of vandalism."

"That's . . ." "Great" didn't seem like the right word to use, in this context. "That's good news," I agreed. "Were there . . ." I took a leap. "I'm guessing you didn't find any connections to Melanie's disappearance?"

He gave me a bemused smile that didn't quite reach his eyes. "Now, Nancy, I know you're our resident child sleuth," he said, presumably trying for "patient" but missing it by a lot.

I tilted my head at him. "I prefer 'detective.'"

Now he *did* smile with his eyes, a slow, condescending grin that slithered over his lips unappealingly. "Sure. Detective. Well, I'll tell you, we've been very grateful for all the help you and your friends have given us"—he shot me a loaded look, reminding me of my reluctance to come forward with the information about the bird when it first happened—"but we'll take it from here. You're right, we still don't know where Melanie is, and while I can't exactly comment on the details of an ongoing investigation, I assure you that we are following any and all leads."

"But I—" I needed to tell him about the fairgrounds. But the writing on my windshield—that was—

What, a hallucination?

Well, it was unreliable at best. But the grass, that was real, a concrete, tangible thing. Even Daisy and Lena had seen it. And for once, that total-transparency switch had been flipped in a way that would not be ignored. At last.

"But nothing," he said, cutting me off. "I have to get down

to the station. I have some questions for Ms. Mark, as I'm sure you'll understand."

"We have something to report!" Lena blurted. "There was more vandalism. Someone burned a note into the grass at the fairgrounds—a warning."

McGinnis tilted his chin at that, curious. "Really?"

"Yes," I said, locking eyes with him.

"Well, that's definitely useful information," he said. "I thank you for bringing it to our attention. My men and I will be looking into that."

"That's—that's it?" I sputtered, stunned and frustrated. "You don't want to ask us about it?"

He shrugged. "You told us you saw something at the fairgrounds. We'll check it out." He leaned closer to me. "Don't you get it, Nancy? For me, this isn't some silly little high school puzzle to solve. This is actually my job—my *duty*. And believe it or not, I know how to do my job. I'm very good at it."

"Of course," I snapped. Barely seventeen and I'd already learned the hard way that very few people in the world enjoyed being in any way shown up by a puny little *girl*.

Too bad for them.

Because I *also* was very good at what I did. And what I did, as McGinnis so deprecatingly put it, was solve puzzles.

Maybe he didn't want my help, beyond the occasional tip or point in the right direction. But he was going to get it anyway. Just because Caroline Mark had been clinched as a suspect didn't mean the case was closed. Melanie was still missing.

Was her disappearance related to Caroline's vandalism? Was it connected to the warning in the grass? And *had* someone been following me the other night in Stone Ridge?

The biggest looming question, hanging over me, heavier, even, than a noose:

What was the Naming Day curse, and were we all falling victim to it, even as preparations for the festival churned on?

CHAPTER SIXTEEN

Parker: Lunch?

Nancy: Yes, please.

Nancy: On my way to the cafeteria. Save me a seat?

Parker: And a mystery meat nugget.

Nancy: Not to seem like an ingrate, but that I could probably actually do without.

Parker: Don't knock it until you try it!

Parker: Fine, have it your way.

Nancy: That's generally my preference.

Parker: Mine, too. Guess we're a perfect match.

A perfect match, I mused, looking over Parker's last text message, *or a perfect storm*? After all, two people who were accustomed to each having their own way were bound to butt heads sooner or later, right?

I'd worry about that another time, though. I had plenty on my mind as it was.

In my head, time had ground to a standstill since McGinnis had carted Caroline away (sans handcuffs, of course, but a cart-off was still a cart-off, and I knew it when I saw it). In reality, though, for the most part, life went on. The case was gnawing at me—as, I suspected, it must have also been for Melanie's family and friends. But for those who hadn't been directly impacted by the vandalism, and who hadn't been present when a bird slammed itself directly into the newsroom window bearing a decidedly downbeat missive, things were basically business as usual, especially now that Caroline had been pinned down as a perp. Now all the chief had to do was find Melanie, and fresh off the success of having collared Caroline, that felt—to others, apparently, anyway—eminently within reach.

It all seemed way too neat and tidy for me.

I was walking down the hall toward the cafeteria, stomach grumbling, when I heard voices. I was running late and the halls were mostly deserted, which meant the sound was isolated, my awareness heightened.

It was a guy and a girl. Arguing.

Typical teen drama, I assumed, planning to continue on my way as my stomach gave another misguided rumble. But then I realized, *I know that voice*, and I paused in my tracks.

It was Theo. And he sounded *testy*.

"Look, I'm sorry things worked out the way they did, but you have no right to blame me. You dug your own grave."

You dug your own grave. It was only a figure of speech, but it made the fine hairs on the back of my neck stand at attention.

"You didn't have to sic Barney Fife on me, though, did you?" The girl, also tense. Which was how I was accustomed to hearing her. *Caroline.*

I inched closer to the corner of the hallway, flattening myself against the row of lockers as best I could, hoping to get a better listen.

"Come on. The guy had a 'long list' of exactly two people: you and me. We were the only ones around here that had publicly opposed the reenactment. If I hadn't pointed him in your direction, he would have ended up sniffing around me. Girl— you *were* guilty!"

"Well, you couldn't have him sniffing around, could you?" she snapped, her voice dripping with scorn.

"Caroline, you did all those things. You can't exactly get all high and mighty in this scenario. I'm sorry, but you're gonna have to deal."

Emotion washed over me, hot and high. Caroline *was* responsible, at least for some of the stuff that'd been happening. I couldn't hold back. I stormed around the corner, coming face-to-face with Theo, and shocking both of them.

"Nancy, jeez," Theo said. "Lurk much?"

I shot him a look. "See, the thing is, lurking generally pays off, I've learned." I whirled to face Caroline, anger flooding my system. This was the person who'd trashed Daisy's locker after all. That made this more than criminal, more than potentially violent. That made this *personal*. "They let you go? Already?"

"I'm still a minor. It's vandalism. It was a first offense. My parents spoke to McGinnis; I'm going to pay a fine and do some community service. Believe it or not, I actually have to help set up the stage at the fairground." She made a retching sound. "I guess McGinnis thought it was very 'let the punishment fit the crime,' all tragically ironic and such."

"That's not irony," I said bitterly.

"No one ever knows how to use that word correctly," Theo said, apparently completely unfazed by the entire scene.

"We can save the English lesson for later," I said. "First offense. So he counted the locker, the newsroom, and the raven together. Like a three-for-one. I guess you're just lucky he hadn't seen the burned grass at the fairgrounds when he first questioned you. The punishment could have been way worse."

"Yeah, they could've insisted you do makeup for the show, too," Theo put in sarcastically.

I looked at him. "Not helpful."

Caroline, meanwhile, stared at me. "I had nothing to do with that raven. *Or* the fairgrounds. I promise."

I put my hands on my hips. "And I suppose you weren't following me the other night, over by Stone Ridge, either?" Following me, and leaving creepy-as-hell messages on my windshield.

She flushed, and dropped her gaze. "Sorry," she mumbled. "I, uh . . . well, I kept hoping that if I mentioned the curse, like, dwelled on it, you know, people would get spooked and back off, maybe cancel Naming Day entirely. But it turns out, no one knows very much about the curse in the first place, so getting people riled up was, like, a very tall order."

"Yeah," I said simply. "That curse has a very slight footprint. It's definitely a thing." I sympathized with her—but only to a point. She had terrorized me down a dark and twisty road, after all. It hadn't done much to engender goodwill. (Although it *did* rule Parker out, which was a relief.)

"Look," she said, cocking her hip and looking me in the eye again. "You came to talk to me about my alibi, about being with Stephenson—"

"Right," I said, remembering. "Wait—he lied for you?"

She shrugged, her cheeks pink.

"Why would he do that?" I demanded. When her cheeks blazed red and she averted her gaze, I realized. *"Oh."* My eyes widened. "Caroline, you have to tell someone."

"It's not like that." She paused, taking a deep breath. "Or, okay, maybe it's *kind* of like that. Or, I kind of want it to be. *Wanted.* I mean, it just made it all the more humiliating that he didn't cast me."

No wonder Caroline had been so furious.

I stepped forward, reaching out to her. "Caroline, you know that's—"

"I know," she said, nodding and cutting me off. "I know. And believe me, Stephenson *definitely* knows. Whatever was going on—and I'll admit, I have . . . *had* . . . feelings, and I definitely felt like it was mutual. . . ." I must have shuddered, or otherwise reacted, because a flicker of defensiveness crossed her face.

NANCY DREW: THE CURSE ~ 189

"Anyway, whatever it was, trust me, we *both* know. It was wrong. And nothing ever happened. It was all totally emotional."

"Good," I said simply. Did I believe her? Maybe. She *wanted* to be telling me the truth, that was clear. But I wasn't her mother, or her guidance counselor, and picking this story apart further wasn't going to ingratiate me to her, or make her any more willing to trust me or tell me the truth.

"Anyway," she said, "you were investigating the whole thing, that much was obvious. And, well . . ." She trailed off, suddenly shy. "Anyone who's ever heard your name knows you're, like, *known* for investigating. So if *anyone* could get to the bottom of the curse thing, it was you."

"So you followed me to that interview in Stone Ridge." Well, that explained the overwhelming feeling I'd had of being watched. I *was* being watched.

"But you came up empty," I said, "just like I did."

"Yeah." She did sound genuinely remorseful. I wasn't sure where that got us now, but I noted it nonetheless.

I stared at her. "Why did you do it? All of it?"

"It was Daisy," she said. "She was the one. She's in the reenactment, she's on the paper, her family is Old Horseshoe Bay—"

"Old as it gets," Theo agreed, as if to remind us that he was still here. Not that there was any great *need* for him to still be here. But then again, I was actually the intruder, having inserted myself into Theo and Caroline's conversation in the first place. So I gave him the most patient, if strained, smile I could muster.

"That's why I targeted her," Caroline said. "It wasn't cool, but it seemed like the best way to, you know, make a thing."

"A thing." I hated the idea that *my* friend had been targeted for Caroline's petty revenge scheme, but standing here in front of her, processing the waves of humiliation radiating off of her . . . it was hard not to feel the tiniest bit sorry for her.

I opened my mouth to say something—though what, I wasn't sure yet. But before I could get a word out, Lena came dashing up to me. Her typically styled hair was frizzing around her in a fuzzy halo, and her eyes were red-rimmed, mascara forming sooty rings under her eyes. In a word, she looked manic. I felt my heart squeeze—what next?

"Parker said you were on your way to the caf!" she managed, her voice thick. "I was looking for you there."

"What is it?" I asked.

"It's Daisy!" she said, breaking into a hysterical sob.

"What?" An ice block slid down my spine. "What about Daisy?"

She gave another sob, this one more guttural, raw. She looked at me, grabbing me tightly by the shoulders.

"She's gone now too."

PART THREE

THE CURSE

The year was 1942. The Japanese had just bombed Pearl Harbor, and the US was preparing to send its boys off to join the war. And while Horseshoe Bay often feels like a place frozen in time, for once, that wasn't to be the case.

When the first round of letters arrived, including one for Hugo Dewitt, not a year out of Keene High at the time, his fiancée, like so many of those of the time, swore she'd wait for him.

But for Hugo Dewitt's betrothed—and so many others—it was to be a wait that would never end.

While the rest of the town went on to celebrate Naming Day in ignorant bliss, those boys from Horseshoe Bay went off to fight a war—and never returned. The letters arrived a week later, leaving their families to lament that they'd been celebrating their town's history while their boys were dying on its behalf.

It wasn't the first tragedy to coincide with Naming Day. It wasn't even the most notable, the most spectacular, or the most cruel.

It wasn't the last, either.

People don't speak of the Naming Day curse. But it's no secret this town's most joyous tradition has also been met with some of our most tragic losses.

Why should this Naming Day be any different?

Hence my sworn promise to you, today: It shouldn't. And it won't.

CHAPTER SEVENTEEN

In moments of panic, there's that beautiful old cliché about time seeming to stand still. I'd always assumed it was just an expression. Kind of like *to dig one's own grave*. And maybe, technically, it *was* just an expression. Maybe what I was experiencing was no more a temporal fold or a hiccup in the metaphysical fabric of life than it was a singular hallucination, a total system shutdown on the part of my body at hearing the horrific, unfathomable news.

A girl can dream.

But this wasn't a dream; it was a nightmare.

I watched as Lena's mouth continued to form words, but I heard none of them. The air seemed to leave the room, and my vision tunneled to a tiny pinpoint, like I was standing at the bottom of a long-abandoned well. Faintly, indistinct as something murmured underwater, vague words began to swim toward me.

Note . . . missing . . . I heard them on some basic, primal level, but couldn't process them, couldn't knit them together into any semblance of understanding.

There was something else down here with me too.

Something putrid, musty.

I reached up and rubbed my fingers across my neck, not at all surprised to find myself touching a frayed rope. A noose.

There, at the bottom of this odd psychic well, wrapped in wooly bunting, I found a noose draped around my neck.

Trance Nancy . . . Dream Nancy . . . whoever this girl was? Somehow, she wasn't surprised.

I felt Lena's frantic hands on my arms again, gripping me tightly enough to pull me out of the well and back into the hall of the high school. Her mouth, in real time now, shouted as she shook me.

"Nancy? Can you hear me?" Another shake. "Do you hear what I'm saying, Nancy? She's missing! *Nancy!*" Her voice rose, becoming hoarser with each plea. "Are you listening?"

Something about the pitch of her tone, beyond panic and verging on total hysteria, finally broke the spell. The well, the horseshoe, the darkness—they were all gone, though that smell of must and decay still wafted, lingering. I was firmly in the hallway of Keene High, and Daisy was . . .

"Missing?" I swayed for a minute, a little woozy on my feet. Lena was still holding my arms, and I clung to her.

"Are you *sure*?" I asked, slowly coming back into my body. But of course she was sure. Lena wasn't the kind who would freak out like this without damn good (or bad, given the circumstances) cause.

"I found a note. The . . . kidnapper must have left it. In my backpack. I don't . . . I have no idea when it was left. How could I have missed it? *How did I miss it, Nancy?*"

Now it was my turn to coax Lena back from the edge. Tears welled in her eyes. I could count on one hand the number of times I'd seen Lena cry. "You just did. It's okay. You didn't do this." I took her hand. "But you have to show me the note."

"Maybe I didn't do this." She shook her head. "But I definitely didn't do anything that could have prevented it either."

"That makes two of us." Though I *had* tried, I thought fiercely. I had looked into the curse as best I could, with so little to go on. The push and pull of how and when my secrets served me best was going to make me insane if I let it.

Still, though. "I have to see the note."

"Here." She gave it to me, unfolding it carefully and pressing it flat with her fist against the face of a locker.

I looked at it. Typed and printed, lettering in standard black, nothing at all distinguishing about the paper or ink. Anyone with a laptop, a printer, and a ream of paper could have done this.

The curse lives. Call off Naming Day if you want to see Daisy Dewitt returned.

Alive.

It was utterly nondescript. But I snapped a picture of it on my phone, for good measure.

I shuddered. With Melanie's disappearance, the lack of notes or clues of any kind meant we could retain a drop of denial, if we wanted. No one had claimed the abduction or asked for ransom. This, on the other hand, couldn't have been clearer. Daisy was being held captive. Someone wanted Naming Day canceled badly enough that they were willing to resort to kidnapping to get it done.

"Lena," I said, looking up. "We have to take this to the chief. And Daisy's parents."

"Nancy." Lena's voice softened. She smiled at me, slightly incredulous. "Are you kidding me? I already have."

I needed to think. We'd been dismissed from school early—that was my mom's suggestion in her professional capacity as crisis counselor.

Apparently, two missing students constituted a *major* crisis, and Principal Wagner was about as worried about a major crisis at her school as the rest of us were about the actual missing students. McGinnis, Principal Wagner, and the mayor had called for an emergency town hall meeting tomorrow night, Friday, but incredibly, in the meantime, the Naming Day celebration had still not *actually* been canceled, so Lena went off to work on floats that we all secretly suspected were never going to be seeing any kind of parade. She was reluctant but admitted in the end that it was better than sitting around wondering where—and *how*—Daisy was.

"I'm on it," I promised her, meaning it, but going just as crazy, all the same. "I'll keep you posted."

I'd spent the afternoon digging around online, hoping against hope that there was some random clue about the Naming Day curse just lurking, waiting for the click of my fingers. There wasn't. Finally, frustrated, I'd grabbed my notebook and wandered to town, heading down Main Street.

I'd *also* spent the afternoon negotiating a flurry of concerned texts from Parker; it was definitely sweet, but Daisy was basically the only thing on my mind. This case was too open-ended; having no real suspects was just as stressful as having too many—and much less useful, too.

The sun had just begun to set, fiery orange streaks flashing against the gray-white of the evening sky. In the distance, I heard the caw of a bird—something large, the sound echoing and ominous.

The dead raven flashed in my mind, neck twisted and eyes unseeing, a few droplets of blood spattering the grass where it lay. Something about it still nagged at the corner of my mind, a loose thread from a sweater that was slowly unraveling.

Or maybe I was the one unraveling.

The trees around me seemed to twist in the moonlight; twisted, gnarled branches became limbs, beckoning.

Warning me.

Shivering, I settled myself into the pagoda at the edge of the town square, overlooking the bluff. When I breathed in I could taste the salt air, and the spray of the ocean tickled my skin even from up here, up high. Normally, the pagoda was a peaceful spot, good for thinking, reviewing notes, clearing my head. But tonight, the empty square felt foreboding, and I knew that if my parents had any idea I was out here, alone, with two classmates missing, they wouldn't be happy.

They knew I could take care of myself, but there was no reason to go tempting fate. That was what they'd say.

Idly, I took out my phone. A bunch of posts from Keene High's social media were waiting for me. Since the bird and all the subsequent weirdness, I hadn't had much use for Instagram. But Lena had continued to post—she'd had to, of course. I scrolled through the images, overwhelmed to see how the rest of the school was carrying on while for so many of us, life was completely turned inside out. Here was a shot of the reenactment rehearsal, the cast goofing around in ratty old-timey wigs. Here was Parker and some guys from the soccer team, posing with different tools in front of the skeleton of a parade float. I grinned at that, wishing I'd been able to join him. I liked that he'd kept his word even after he knew I wouldn't be keeping mine, that day.

An older one, now: Melanie, giving a brilliant smile and holding out her script.

Suddenly, I heard a crackle—a leaf crunching, a twig snapping. I jumped up and whirled around, desperately scanning the area for any sign of life. But the square was still absolutely deserted.

A ghost town. I shivered. Another one of those figures of speech.

Crackle. I heard it again. Footsteps, I was sure of it.

"Hello?" I called, feeling foolish. But not foolish enough not to do it in the first place. Paranoia has saved me more times than I care to count.

Silence.

Another caw of a bird, this one sending a flicker of memory through my mind, or was it just remnants of that horrible nightmare?

Wide-planked floors. Deep-throated caws. The shadow of a broad, strong wingspan. The echo of a man's voice, clear and commanding.

What the hell was that? I could see it, hear it, even *smell* it— wood chips, manure—so clearly.

But I couldn't quite grab it in my mind, couldn't put my finger on what, exactly, I was recalling. Or if it was even real in the first place.

Wham.

I tried to scream, but thick fingers closed over my eyes, my mouth.

Darkness.

Was this the last thing Daisy saw too?

I bucked, trying to throw whoever it was off, straining to make a sound against the hands.

"Whoa!"

I recognized that voice.

"Nancy!"

Parker?

Slowly, my pulse returned to normal and the adrenaline that had spiked through me seemed to dissipate.

202 ~ MICOL OSTOW

The hands unpeeled and turned me around, and then we were face-to-face. He looked baffled.

"Nancy, it's me. Sorry if I scared you."

"*If* you scared me?" I gave him a look, trying to keep it light. It wasn't easy with my heart still thudding in my chest. "Creeping up behind me? What were you *trying* to do?"

He flushed. "Um, I promise you, I wasn't trying to . . . creep. Sorry about that. I swear, I thought it would be cute. I wanted to do the whole *guess who?* thing. But then you freaked out."

"Yeah, I guess I get a little jumpy when I'm alone in a deserted square overlooking a bluff, and my best friend's been kidnapped," I pointed out, hating the edge in my voice, even if it was totally warranted.

He winced. "I hear you. It was a bad idea. Terrible joke, as far as jokes go. I promise you, I won't ever try to be cute again."

He looked so woebegone, and my initial shock had already begun to wear off. It was hard to stay annoyed, even if he *had* exhibited *profoundly* bad judgment. "Well, that's just it—you don't need to *try* to be cute. You just are, naturally." I showed him the Instagram feed I'd been stalking. "Look, there you are, being cute."

"Aw." He smiled. "Forgiven, then?"

"Forgiven," I agreed, stepping closer to him. I took his hands and pulled him to me, kissing him gently.

After we pulled apart, I looked at him. "Honestly, I'm just relieved it was you and not Caroline again. That was my first thought."

He frowned. "Caroline *again*?"

Hmm. Did I not mention that to him?

"Oh, you know." I laughed, waving it off. "I was . . . out the other day, investigating a little bit. . . . It turned out she was following me."

"Wait." His eyes narrowed. I could see the sharp set of his brow, even in the moonlight. "Caroline Mark was *following you*?"

I shrugged. "Apparently. She confirmed it just this morning, as a matter of fact."

He grabbed me by the wrists, pulling me down to sit on the pagoda bench. "Nancy, what the hell?"

I filled him in as quickly as possible—admittedly, trying to downplay the situation as much as I could in response to his panic.

"I can handle Caroline Mark," I assured him. "I've dealt with worse."

"I can't say that makes me feel that much better," he said.

I tried to tell myself that it was sweet, the way he was so worried about me.

But the thing is, Parker: It's not my job to make you *feel better about* my *investigations.*

I didn't say it, though.

"Maybe you should, I don't know, back off from investigating for a while?" he suggested, tracing circles on the inside of my wrist with his finger.

I felt a twinge in my gut. Was this shades of David—and the

other friends and guys I'd lost over a mystery? "I love that you worry; it's adorable," I started.

Is it, though?

"But you have to understand, investigating is what I do."

"I understand. I do. But Caroline Mark obviously has some stuff to work through," he protested. "She could be dangerous. Not to mention, whoever kidnapped Daisy and Melanie is still out there. It's terrifying."

"I know," I said. Did he not think I knew that? Daisy was my best friend. I was the most terrified of all. "Which is why I need to do everything in my power to solve the case as quickly as I can." I looked at him. "Is that going to be a problem for you?"

He sighed heavily. "I mean, they say the future is female, right?"

I didn't *love* the slightly joking tone to his voice there. "I think I saw that on a mug somewhere," I replied carefully.

"Girls who kick ass are hot, right?"

"I like to think so."

"So, yeah: This isn't a problem. Go forth and kick ass. Solve the case."

"I'm going to," I said.

He brushed my hair back from my face gently then, and leaned in for another kiss. I obliged, but even as my stomach swirled in excitement at his nearness, darker thoughts crowded my mind. Parker *said* I should solve the case, that he wouldn't stand in my way. But I didn't need his permission. And I knew too that there were plenty of girls out there who would have found his protective vibe super chivalrous. But deep down, I had to admit to myself: I wasn't one of those people who thought that the "future" was female. We were here *now*. I was here *now*.

And if Parker was going to be all alpha male about it?

Well, maybe that wasn't a problem for him. But I couldn't say the same for myself.

CHAPTER EIGHTEEN

Friday

If the town square had been curiously empty the night before, then every single Horseshoe Bay resident was making up for it now. I had never in my life seen town hall as packed as it was for Chief McGinnis's emergency meeting. Everyone was on high alert and taking the disappearances seriously. It was a relief to know we were all, finally, on the same page, even if it was a terrible page in a book I truly wished I weren't reading. It made the chances of finding Daisy and Melanie soon, better. And maybe someone—anyone—would have another piece of information about the history of the Naming Day curse.

Basically, the entire town had been crushed into the hall, my parents and me in the very front row, Mom to my right and Dad to my left, each holding one hand so tightly I thought they'd cut off my circulation soon enough. Mom's eyes were red, and Dad's jaw was tight. Both were deeply worried about Daisy. Lena was here too, with her parents, somewhere in the melee. Though I couldn't see them, I knew they were just as upset. Parker as well.

The room was hot, and the air was tense. A long table had been set up on the stage where the chief, Principal Wagner, and the mayor—a woman of about the same age (and the same demeanor) as the principal—all sat, a pitcher of water sweating condensation droplets all over the white tablecloth that had been spread on the table. Daisy's parents were up there too, her mother's eyes red-rimmed and welling with tears that constantly threatened to spill over. Her father looked stern, stoic, but I suspected he was hanging on by a thread. Mostly, the mere fact of their presence had set an ominous tone for this meeting: the black wool clothes, the drawn expressions, the gravity of their importance in Horseshoe Bay . . .

And the fact that their daughter was missing.

They weren't the only ones up on the stage. Another man and woman sat at the very edge of the table, both pale and gaunt. Melanie's parents. A twinge of guilt bit at me. Just because Daisy's abduction had an extra layer of resonance for me personally didn't mean any less as far as these two and their suffering.

We need to find the girls.

I *need to find the girls.*

The urgency came to me, a searing flash of actual, physical pain.

Chief McGinnis reached for the microphone on the table in front of him. He tapped at it to be sure it was on. "Hello," he said, to a burst of static. Everyone in the room reacted, squirming in their seats and flinching.

"Thank you for coming out tonight," he went on. "I know everyone's very worried about recent events and our oncoming Naming Day Festival."

"Call off the festival!" someone shouted from the back of the room, prompting a wave of boos and other protests. It was hard to tell whether people were protesting the Naming Day Festival or the idea of canceling it. As much as no one seemed to want to admit *anything* about a curse, it was hard to imagine straight-up *ignoring* the letter that had shown up when Daisy went missing.

"We understand people are emotional," Mayor Johnson chimed in. Her voice was measured, almost regal, as though she'd somehow absorbed everyone's emotional responses and synthesized them coolly to a more tolerable level.

"Our children are in danger! Who knows who'll be targeted next!" It was a small, mousy woman just a few seats behind me. I recognized her from a few school functions: the PTA treasurer. Her daughter was an equally mousy freshman who'd won the science fair with something to do with osmosis and solar energy.

Onstage, Daisy's mother went sheet white. Her father, meanwhile, slammed a fist down on the table more heavily than a judge banged a gavel. "Our daughter *is* gone!" he bellowed.

"Ours is too!" It was Melanie's mother now, her voice thick with sobs. "Funny how no one thought to call a town hall meeting until the daughter of a *founding family* vanished!"

The booing grew louder now, building to a crescendo. From somewhere behind me, a crumpled ball of paper—the agenda for tonight's discussion?—went soaring overhead. Mom squeezed my hand a little harder. I nestled up against her, grateful to have her here.

The mayor stood, her expression strained now. She held her hand out in a *calm down* gesture. "Please," she said, "we understand why you're all upset. I assure you, we are just as upset, and just as committed to getting your children home." She looked from Melanie's parents to Daisy's. "*Both* of your children."

"The mayor has asked me to be very clear in reiterating the specifics of what we know at present. We have distinct sets of incidents," Chief McGinnis said. He was generally unflappable (if a bit ornery), but in the face of so many hysterical parents, it was clear he wanted to tread lightly. "First: A bird bearing a warning note flew into one of our high school classroom windows. Students initially dismissed the incident as a prank"— and somehow, even amidst the din and crowd, I felt his gaze find me, searing a hole in me like an ant in a magnified sun ray—"and it wasn't reported to us immediately."

Indignant sounds echoed off the walls of the auditorium. I felt a flicker of shame in my belly.

"Second, Daisy Dewitt's locker was vandalized, as was the *Masthead* newsroom. The culprit in both of these incidents was later revealed to be another student at Keene High, who *was*, in fact, playing a prank. She was disgruntled because she hadn't been cast in the reenactment."

Now a sprinkle of laughter broke out amidst the solemn murmurs. I had to feel for Caroline, wherever she was, out there in the auditorium. Even if McGinnis hadn't called her out by name, she was hardly anonymous in this room. She had to be feeling pretty humiliated right about now.

"But then immediately after the locker incident, Melanie Forest was reported missing. Last but not least, Daisy Dewitt was reported missing. A threatening note was found in her friend's locker, and later we found a corroborating note with the exact same message in Daisy's wallet, in her own locker, as well."

Another note? I sat up in my seat. Behind the chief, an overhead projector called up two side-by-side images, one of the note that Lena had found, and one of Daisy's wallet—red, Kate Spade, a stain on the leather from a latte with a faulty to-go lid that she'd never been able to clean off, no matter how many expensive products she tried. It lay flat on a table next to an evidence bag, a note exactly like Lena's just beside it.

My throat tightened, and my head felt hot. I hadn't realized that the chief had gone through Daisy's locker, though of course it made sense, and whatever I'd been expecting to see tonight, it wasn't that. I'd laid eyes on Daisy's wallet probably at least once a day for the last . . . five years? If not longer. In this context, the sight was chilling.

Mom must have read my mind—she was good at that—because she rubbed my back reassuringly.

"Finally," the chief concluded, "shortly before Daisy's disappearance was reported, my officers got a tip about another incident of Naming Day–related vandalism out at the fairgrounds." I felt his eyes on me again, this time more impassive.

"What about the girl—I mean, the *student*," someone piped in from behind me. "The one who was behind the vandalism?"

"We've managed to eliminate that person as a suspect in the matters of the student disappearances, the bird incident, and the fairgrounds," McGinnis said.

I would have killed to know how definitively he'd managed to "eliminate" Caroline, but I didn't think he was lying. I was ninety-nine percent certain that Caroline had had nothing to do with the disappearances, and she'd been straight with me about following me . . . and about other stuff too.

Of course, even being definitive about those two incidents, we still had *missing students* to find.

"Unfortunately, we don't have a lot of leads on Melanie Forest's disappearance," McGinnis went on, prompting Ms. Forest's face to turn a queasy shade of olive. "Though we aren't ruling out the idea of a connection, the fact that Daisy's abductor—"

At the word "abductor," Ms. Dewitt swayed in her chair. Daisy's father wrapped a meaty arm around her, propping her up.

"—left a note with a threat leads me to think there may not be one."

Now Melanie's mother let forth with a guttural wail, and her husband swiftly escorted her from the stage.

"Please," the mayor said, taking a firm grasp on her own microphone, "we're asking *anyone* who may have any information at all about the missing girls to please come forward. And do offer the Dewitts and the Forests your strength and support in this deeply trying time."

"Pray for us," Daisy's father said simply, his voice booming into his microphone and out into the crowd, a smooth baritone.

"Hopes and prayers? Is that *really* the best we can do?"

This time, it took no time for me to place the voice. It was Theo, of course, clearly downright horrified that the town was hesitating for even a moment on pulling the plug on Naming Day.

"Mr. MacCabe," McGinnis drawled. "You had another idea?"

Theo extricated himself from the front aisle seat he'd been in and moved to the edge of the stage, positioning himself at just the right angle to be able to see the chief and everyone onstage as well as everyone in the crowd, too.

"Call me crazy, guys," he started, his usual sardonic tone rendered an octave or two higher than usual, "but what if we, oh, I don't know . . . *called off Naming Day*?" He threw his hands up. "Someone out there sure wants us to! It definitely couldn't hurt!"

A few more balled-up programs flew toward him, which he dodged awkwardly.

"You can't let 'em win!" someone called out.

Except you can, when your friend's life is at risk.

"But, actually? You can," Theo said, echoing my thoughts. "It's not 'losing' if we get our classmates back." He scanned the crowd, pleading. "Please tell me I'm not the only one in the room who thinks the well-being of actual people is worth more than a dumb *town festival*?"

I flinched. He shouldn't have called it "dumb." Around here, it wouldn't go over well.

"I'm with him." Another voice rang out, and another lanky figure joined Theo at the stage. *Parker.* His eyes found me in the crowd and locked in. "History, tradition . . . whatever— it's all important." His voice caught on the word, like he was *maybe*, just maybe, implying that some of us in this town had histories that weren't as important as we liked to think.

Or maybe you're reading into it.

"But we could probably still stand to be a little cautious," he went on, not taking his eyes from my face. "Actual people's actual lives are at stake."

Okay. Point: Parker.

But no. Coming back to my senses, I gave a sharp shake of my head. Didn't he understand? The fact that Daisy's life was at stake—that just meant I couldn't afford to hold back, couldn't afford a moment's hesitation. I liked Parker desperately, but if I had to choose between him and an investigation, I knew what I'd choose.

"Believe me, this is a matter we've debated at great length amongst those of us up here onstage right now," Principal Wagner said. "We decided that the best course of action would be to take a vote. After all: This is your town. And these are your daughters."

From the wings, Daisy's mother gave a small whimper.

The chief stood. "A show of hands, please. All in favor of carrying on with Naming Day as planned." I twisted in my seat. From just a cursory glance, it was clearly a landslide. Onstage, Melanie's mother's face crumpled, and my own mother's arm tightened on my shoulder.

The opposing faction may have been smaller in number, but their reaction was tremendous. Riotous shouting broke out instantly, and the chief gave a short nod that immediately sent a group of his officers weaving down the aisles with their arms out, aiming to keep the peace.

My father clapped me on the back. "I wish I could say I was surprised. This town . . ."

My jaw dropped. "But . . . that's it?" My eyes filled with hot tears. "Dad, we can't just, just—leave this way! It's *Daisy*!"

He sighed. "Believe me, sweetie, I know. And I wish there were something else I could do right now."

"Talk to him," I begged, my voice cracking. "Say something to McGinnis. He'll listen to you."

Dad gave me a half-hearted smile. "I think you overestimate my powers of charm and persuasion, hon. Or you underestimate the influence his constituents have over him. Either way, this isn't over yet. You know Daisy's parents won't rest until she's found."

"Melanie, too," I said. "I mean, obviously Daisy's the one that's legitimately driving me crazy, but Melanie's in danger too. Her mom was right. It's gross the way that the chief didn't think to amp up his investigation until a *Dewitt* went missing."

"Nancy," my father said, his voice calm, "I know you're upset and worried about your friend. And I don't blame you. I'm worried too, I promise you. But another reason that the search may have escalated when Daisy vanished? Not only her last name, but the fact that at that point, there were *two* girls missing."

I gave him a look. "Okay, sure. Use *logic*."

He kissed me on the forehead. "Let's get home. Preparations for Naming Day will go on—"

"Ridiculous," I huffed, crossing my arms over my chest.

"Maybe so," he offered, "but your mom and I are on the case. The whole town is, even those who raised their hands in favor of carrying on with Naming Day."

Traitors. I glanced at the stage. Theo was still up there, looking agitated, but now he was joined by a girl—Anna, Caroline's friend from the quad, who I knew was in Drama Club with Melanie, Caroline, and Daisy. Whatever she was saying to him—it was too crowded for me to read her lips—it seemed to calm him down well enough. After a minute, he walked off with her, his shoulders slumped and his head down.

Dad grabbed my hand and squeezed it. His hand was warm, his grip, comforting. "We'll find them, Nancy," he said. "I promise."

I nodded. My father didn't break promises. It was one of the amazing-est of his many amazing qualities.

But this time, he wouldn't even need to worry about it.

Because there was someone else on the case too:

Me.

CHAPTER NINETEEN

Saturday

They come at daybreak.

"Of course, if you train them, they'll come any time you holler, but it's best if they're trained. Otherwise, before you know it, they have a mind of their own.

"And no one wants that.

"One needs . . . obedience."

I want to ask, Who are you? but I'm in the dream again, submerged, deep within the nightmare, wide-planked floors beneath my bare feet, an open window, a curtain dancing in the breeze. . . .

The acrid, sickly sweet scent of rot, a trace of . . . manure? Yes, manure, like I smelled in the town square the other night.

You're forgetting something, Nancy. Something important. Some detail that is the key to everything that's unraveled since . . .

I freeze. In the dream, I know.

The ravens are coming again.

They come at daybreak.

Or so I hear.

And now they come again. For me.

I woke up, gasping, to the chirp of morning birds. Not a sound I usually equate with terror, but maybe there were new rules in this new, post-Daisy world.

I shuddered. *Don't even think it, Drew.*

She's not gone. Because you're *going to find her.*

You're forgetting something, Nancy. The idea had come to me—no, the certainty. I could definitely upgrade it from "idea" to "certainty." But regardless, there was something I was missing.

The irony, though, was that knowing I was forgetting something did nothing to spur a memory.

I stepped out of bed and wrapped myself in a cozy robe, hoping that it would be comforting in a way that my thoughts weren't. It only semi-worked. More comforting was the sound of the coffee maker as I padded downstairs. Mom and Dad were in the kitchen, the newspaper disassembled and strewn everywhere.

"Morning, hon," Mom said, looking up as I padded into the room. She smiled, but concern was etched into her features. "Did you sleep okay?"

That smell . . . the beating of birds' wings.

I gave her my brightest look, the opposite of how I felt. "I did. Why?"

She gave a slight frown. "Nothing, really . . . I just . . . thought I'd heard you talking in your sleep."

"Must've been dreaming." I fixed a cup of coffee in my favorite mug, which didn't say THE FUTURE IS FEMALE, but it did prominently feature a smiling and capable Rosie the Riveter, and that definitely felt on theme. I sat down at the table and took a sip, trying not to look too contemplative in front of my parents. Didn't want to worry them. More.

"Didn't sound like a very pleasant dream. But if you don't remember it, I guess it couldn't have been that big of a deal." She slid a plate of toast my way, and I plucked a slice up, crunching into it delicately.

Snap. The sound, improbably, reminded me of the crackle of the leaves as I sat in the town square pagoda. Even knowing now that it was only Parker, that sensation of being watched came over me again, viscous as an oil slick, and I shuddered. I set the toast back down and nudged the plate away.

"You sure you're all right?" Now it was Dad, peering at me curiously. "You look a little . . . peaked."

"Oh, stop," I said, pretending to blush. "Flattery will get you everywhere."

"Leave your poor parents alone," Mom said. "Yes, we worry. So sue us. These are worrying times; we reserve the right to hover."

I swallowed. *And here I'd managed to go three whole minutes without thinking about Daisy.* "Hover away. . . ."

Slowly, my eyes lit on something. It was Dad's wallet, resting on the shelf beneath the landline we still kept mounted to the wall, though I didn't think anyone had used that phone since before I was born. The shelf was basically a landing pad for essentials: keys, cash, cell phones . . . so it wasn't strange to see Dad's wallet tossed there.

It wasn't *strange* . . . but it did jostle something in my mind. Was it . . . could it be . . . a thread?

Wallet? I thought back to the town hall meeting. Chief McGinnis had said that a note was found in Daisy's wallet . . . which his team had found in her locker. That all tracked. In a million years, Daisy wouldn't have left her wallet in her locker voluntarily . . . so it stood to reason that the left-behind object was definite evidence of her having been taken.

No one had found any note from Melanie, nor mentioned any clues. The only indication that she'd gone missing was her not showing up to meet with Theo . . . and then her subsequent absence.

Yes, she was gone. No, she hadn't necessarily been taken by the same people . . . or under the same circumstances as Daisy had.

If Melanie's wallet hadn't been left behind, then what *had*? I had to know.

I stood from the table abruptly. "Gotta run," I said, taking a last gulp of coffee. "I just realized there's something I need from the school."

"Naming Day stuff?" Mom asked. "The costumes are ready, by the way. If you want you can take them with you now and drop them off."

"Thanks," I said, leaning down to give her a quick kiss. "I will."

* * *

Daisy's locker had been cordoned off as a crime scene, but a pair of latex gloves and my lock-picking kit and I was in, no problem. The good news was, my nightmare meant I'd woken early enough that even with all the Naming Day prep soon to be happening all over town, the halls at school were completely deserted. I glanced at my watch; *probably not for much longer, though*. If I was going to do this, it had to be now.

Daisy's original padlock had been cut by the police, but they'd put on a new one after, for safekeeping, I guessed. I held my breath for a moment while my lockpick jiggled in the keyhole, but after a second it gave a satisfying *click*, leaving me to take another deep breath before opening my missing friend's locker to have a search of my own.

It was like stumbling onto a rapture scenario. Before me was Daisy's life, as of two days ago, frozen in time. I gasped, unprepared for the flood of emotions that came over me.

Daisy's bag, which would have held her wallet, was a deep gray leather that converted from a messenger bag to a backpack depending on her mood. Magnet photo frames on the inside of the door held up photo-booth shots of Daisy, Lena, and me singing karaoke (badly) at a Chinese restaurant outside of town that hosted theme nights. If I closed my eyes, I could remember that particular evening: The theme was the eighties. The three of us had our hair in teased-up high ponytails and wore fishnet fingerless gloves. We had dim sum, spare ribs, and soup dumplings that I could still taste if I tried hard enough.

Another photo, this one of her and Cooper at homecoming,

her in her cheer costume and him with eye black running in sweaty smudges. We'd won that game. How was Cooper dealing? I wondered.

I sniffed and realized a tear was running down my face.

No time to get mushy, Drew. There was work to do. But this detour down memory lane reminded me of what I was working for, if nothing else.

One thing a good detective and a good actor have in common? They both know it's all about motivation.

Daisy's locker was exactly as I'd expected it to be, down to the lingering scent of tuberose from the Michael Kors perfume she doused herself in every morning. It was painful to confront, but it was what it should have been.

Now to have a peek at Melanie's.

More police tape, another padlock. Another opportunity to break out my lock-picking kit.

Like riding a bike.

Melanie's locker door gave a smooth *click* and opened for me like a book.

If Daisy's had been a rapture scene, this was . . . postapocalyptic? No, that was too harsh, suggesting a wake of destruction. What I found inside of Melanie's locker was the opposite of that. In fact, it was basically the opposite of everything, of anything.

It was completely and totally empty.

Melanie hadn't left a note behind.

She hadn't left *anything* behind.

Did she just happen to have an extremely thorough kidnapper? I wondered. *Or were her circumstances different than Daisy's?*

It wasn't really a question.

I felt a tap on my shoulder and jumped.

"Nancy, relax!" It was Lena, holding her hands up—*sorry, my bad*. Parker was with her. "It's just us."

"What are you guys doing here?" I asked. "It's crazy early."

"Practically the whole town is up. Naming Day Festival is here!" Faked enthusiasm that Lena punctuated with an eye roll. "Half the high school is over at the fairgrounds, working to get the sets and stages up."

"The reenactment," I breathed. "It'll be today."

"In theory, yes," Lena said. "Though given how badly *someone* out there doesn't want it to happen, I kind of can't believe it myself. It seems reckless."

"Phoebe Keller was Daisy's understudy, right?" Was it possible we were overlooking the most obvious suspect there was? It would be cliché, but it would be a relief to solve this case.

Parker looked at me. "I see where you're going with this, but no. When I talked to Phoebe, she said she *doesn't* want to go on. She doesn't feel comfortable taking Daisy's part. She's on Team No Naming Day, it turns out."

"You . . . talked to Phoebe?" I felt a little charge: a thrill that he'd had the same impulse I'd had. Followed swiftly by a prick of annoyance that he'd followed that impulse without me.

With Parker, it felt like I'd finally met my match.

Was it possible that wasn't actually such a good thing?

I shook my head, trying to dislodge the thought. "Team No Naming Day, huh? We could probably stand to have a few more of those around. Although, if McGinnis insists on pushing forward, it could work in my favor and draw the kidnapper out." *If he doesn't kill Daisy first.* I pushed the thought away. "So, who ended up taking her part?"

Lena frowned. "I don't know. Maybe no one. I mean—I think Stephenson might have done a quick rewrite so the part was cut completely."

"I'd approve . . . if it didn't feel slightly ominous."

"So what are you looking for here?" Parker asked. "And how badly is McGinnis going to kick your ass when he sees you trespassing on his crime scene?"

"Ah," I said, "but see, that's why I do it when he isn't around. So he *can't* see." I tapped my forehead. "Always one step ahead." *Also? I've conveniently got my family-friend-slash-detective, Karen, looking out for me. Not that it's a privilege I'm looking to abuse.*

"Cute. But really. Did you find anything?"

"In Daisy's locker, yes. I found *everything.* It's like she literally vanished into thin air. Which obviously makes sense, if she was abducted, because the kidnapper wasn't going to be too worried about making sure she had her pics of her besties singing old-school Madonna over soup dumplings."

Lena's eyes brightened, shiny with nostalgic tears. "She still had that picture up?"

I nodded. *"Has."* I was firm. "She's not gone. Well—I mean, she *is* gone, but it's not permanent. We can't be using past tense."

"You're right." She pointed. "Melanie's locker?"

"Melanie's locker is exactly the opposite of Daisy's—as in, picked clean, not a trace of Melanie left behind. As if *someone* had time to clean it . . . and reason to do so."

"What kind of reason? Whoever took Melanie wants to make sure she keeps up with her trig homework?" Parker asked.

"That's one theory." Personally, I had my own. But I was going to do a little more digging before offering an opinion.

"So, are you almost done, then?" Parker asked. He shifted toward me, and I could feel his hope through the air.

"Not . . . really?" I could tell it wasn't the answer he was hoping for. I wanted to reach out and comfort him, but something stopped me. It was my best friend missing. *I* was the one in need of comfort.

"You're not coming with us to the fairgrounds?" Lena asked, looking truly disappointed.

"I can't." I gestured vaguely at the locker, but she understood.

"Do you want us to stick around? We could help," Parker offered.

"Thanks," I said. "But actually, it would be more helpful if you could go back to the fairgrounds as per your original plan. I'm going to need you to be my eyes and ears on the ground while I follow this lead."

"What lead?" Lena asked. "There's nothing in there."

"That's kind of the point," I said. "I promise, I'll explain later. But in the meantime, can you cover for me? Keep a lookout? If the kidnapper—or whoever is behind *all* the different weird things going on—is going to do something big, today would be the day. They could catch us by surprise no matter how much we may think we're all on high alert."

"If you really think that," Parker said, concern etched across his forehead, "*why* do you insist on keeping at this?"

"For the same reason you talked to Phoebe," I said. "This is a mystery that needs solving." I shrugged. "I know it's stressful. But it's what I do."

He looked to Lena, who nodded. "If it's any consolation, she's very good at it."

"Okay," he said, exhaling and running a hand through his hair, leaving it adorably tousled. I stood and smoothed it back into place. In turn, he brushed my cheek with his hand. "Keep an eye out and an ear to the ground. We can do that. What else?"

"Actually, there's a bag of costumes sitting in my back seat that my mom just finished up. Can you bring those to the fairgrounds?"

"On it," Lena said.

Parker gave me a kiss. "Text me."

"I will," I promised. "And you guys keep me posted."

Anna Gardner was easy to find. Google gave me her address on the first try. 18 Maiden Lane. When I pulled up, there was only one car in the driveway. I prayed that meant Anna was home alone, though that seemed like a lot to ask for. If I had to, I could find a way to ask the questions I needed to ask while her parents were around. But for once since this whole mess began to unravel, it would be nice to catch a break.

I rang her doorbell, smoothing my shirt out over my jeans self-consciously as I waited for someone to answer the door. For a few excruciating beats, I heard nothing but silence.

Finally, though, the door opened.

A small break. Hallelujah.

It was Anna, looking completely confused by my presence, which was valid. "Um, Nancy Drew?" she asked, blinking. "What are you doing here?"

"Are your parents here?" I asked.

"No, I'm alone . . . ," she said slowly, like she was maybe worried about me. *You and me both, Anna.*

"Oh, okay." That was a relief. Small favor number two. I wondered if I was going to run out soon. There had to be a cap on these things. "And you're not heading off to Naming Day?"

She made a face. "I can't believe they didn't call it off. Only Horseshoe Bay would charge full steam ahead with something like Naming Day even with a girl missing and a kidnapper literally *demanding* we call it off. *Two* girls missing."

"But you're a senior," I said.

She gave me a strange half grin. "And yet."

"So you weren't assigned the reenactment?"

She raised her eyebrows. "That was always more Melanie's thing, all along. I mean, we're in Drama Club together, but she was the one who took it seriously. Without Mel around, I just didn't see the point."

"You know," I said, trying to sound more casual and less abrupt, though it definitely wasn't working, "I saw you talking to Theo last night. At the town hall."

"Lucky you." She gave me a look. "We're friends. We talk."

"The thing is," I went on, "lots of people—Theo included, as a matter of fact—feel really strongly about the festival being called off. Especially if going ahead with it might result in the kidnapped girls not coming back. But you didn't say anything last night."

"A lot of people 'didn't say anything' last night. Almost the whole town came out. If everyone had decided to say something, we'd still be there now." Anna crossed her arms over her chest, defensive.

"True," I said. "But there's also the small, pesky fact that Melanie's locker is completely emptied out, while Daisy's is exactly the mess it was the last time she dumped her stuff in it."

"Please tell me you're going somewhere with this," she said. "Just because I'm not into Naming Day doesn't mean I'm excited to be sitting here having you go all Poirot-in-the-last-chapter-of-the-book exposition-y on me. If I wanted this I'd be binge-watching a crime procedural on Netflix right now."

Ouch. I waited as she fidgeted, pursing her lips. But she didn't close the door in my face, which was as much encouragement as I needed right now.

"So, here's the thing," I said, forging ahead. "The lockers look different, Daisy left a note, and Daisy's family and friends are all totally upset that the fest hasn't been canceled. You, on the other hand, were totally cool, calm, and collected last night, and even seemed to talk Theo down from his soapbox."

"And based on the manic gleam in your eye, I'm guessing you think this 'means something.'" She made air quotes with her fingers, hooking them into sarcastic little claws.

"Their disappearances may have been linked in some kind of thematic way," I said, "but the circumstances were completely different. I'm sure of it. And I'm guessing you are too. Because you know something. You wouldn't be so blasé if you didn't. And whatever it is you know, you told Theo. That's how you were able to get him out of the town hall last night when he was winding up to make an even bigger scene."

She rolled her eyes and gave an enormous sigh, putting a hand on one hip and surveying me. "Okay," she said slowly. "Let's be clear: I'm *not* confirming—or denying—any of this random conspiracy theory."

"Crystal clear. And super helpful."

She shook her head. "What are the odds of you leaving here without getting what you want?"

I gave her my brightest smile. "Three guesses."

"Ugh." She groaned and pushed the door open wider, beckoning me. "Fine, come inside."

I stepped into the hallway. "Should I close the door behind me?"

She shook her head. "No, just wait here for a second. I have to get my bag." She disappeared down the hallway.

"Road trip?" I called after. "Where to?"

Her voice drifted toward me from another room, disembodied. "You'll see," she said. "I don't want to ruin the surprise."

And then she was back, in front of me, bag slung over her shoulder, waving a set of car keys. "I'm driving. You can follow me."

CHAPTER TWENTY

The Dunes Motel was a good ninety minutes outside of Horseshoe Bay, far enough from any view of the ocean to be ironically named, and definitely not in a tongue-in-cheek kind of way either. It was a run-down, ramshackle one-story building, a main office with a weathered sign hanging at an awkward angle in the middle and flanked by five rooms on either side. There were two cars parked in the lot. One was a hatchback that had seen better days—probably around the same time that the motel had been in its prime. The other was one I recognized . . . from the high school parking lot.

I got out of my car and stalked to Anna as she pulled into a parking spot right beside room number three . . . and that incredibly familiar car. A sinking feeling came over me as she slowly rolled down her window.

"You knew," I said accusingly. My voice was flat. "You knew

she was here all this time, and you didn't say anything. What the hell were you thinking?" I couldn't believe it. And I was all too aware that while I was chasing down a fake crisis, the clock was ticking on my friend's real-life threat.

"Look"—she shrugged—"I'm not my friend's keeper. She asked me to stay quiet. So why don't you get off *my* back and confront her yourself?"

I gritted my teeth. "Lead the way."

Anna led the way on the short walk to Melanie's motel room, but she stepped aside to let me do the honors when it was time to knock. I held up a fist to rap—ready to bang that door down—then turned to Anna. "Is she expecting us?"

Anna shook her head. "There was no way she'd answer the door if she knew I'd brought you here. You've kind of got a reputation as, you know . . . a snoop. No offense."

"None taken." *It's actually a compliment. And I totally* am *a snoop.* I knocked.

"Who is it?" After a beat, Melanie's voice echoed out to us, suspicious.

I looked at Anna.

"Mel, it's me," she said, stepping closer to the door.

"Uh, okay . . ." After another minute, I heard the click of a chain lock, and then the door swung open.

It was my second house call of the day. And Melanie seemed about as thrilled to see me as Anna had. Less so.

Girl, you have no idea. If Melanie's disappearance *wasn't* linked to Daisy's, then Daisy was in way more danger than I could have imagined. I didn't have time for these dead ends.

"Hey," I said. "Got a minute?"

Without waiting for a response, I sidled my way in.

The Dune Motel being the furthest thing from a luxury resort, her room would have been stuffy and dismal even if a teen girl hadn't been holing up in it for several days like a recluse tertiary character from a CW drama. The one small window was covered with a blackout shade that didn't fully retract, eliminating the possibility of any natural light finding its way into the space, and the walls were covered in wood paneling that was cracked and splintering. The carpet was industrial-grade, in a shade that I think is actually known as "motel putty." Mysterious stains dotted it, creating an unpleasant connect-the-dots effect leading from the bed to the bathroom.

I wasn't eager to see the bathroom.

I sat in the tiny chair wedged up against the wall, just beneath the window. "What's up?" I asked brightly.

Melanie gave a huff and collapsed on the bed, arranging her willowy limbs so she looked like a graceful if put-upon praying mantis in her den. She was wearing a tracksuit that would have been cute if it weren't clear that she'd been wearing it nonstop since she'd first checked in. There was a stain on the corner of one of its pockets—probably coffee, judging by the various abandoned Styrofoam cups littered across all the available surfaces.

She looked at Anna. "I can't believe you brought her here."

Anna rolled her eyes, defensive. "She figured it out. And, I mean, you're seeing the news. You've got your phone."

"You've got *your phone?*" I asked. "*How* have you not been tracked?" Even if she'd turned location services off, a cursory Google search would have revealed *plenty* of talented hackers out there who would have been able to trace her if she'd kept her phone around.

"I've got *a* phone," she replied. "I know you think you're the only one who knows how to be sneaky, but I'm smart too."

"Clearly," I said, gesturing to the squalid scene around us. "So, that brings us to my next question: *What the hell?*"

She laughed. "You're going to have to be more specific."

"People are worried about you!" I said, frustrated. "If you're seeing the news, then you know: My friend is missing too. And it's looking like she was taken, not just voluntarily staging the world's most depressing personal retreat. You set something in motion, Melanie. Something big."

"Uh-uh." She shook her head. "I didn't set anything in motion. The *raven* set it all off. I just capitalized on the chaos."

"But *why?*"

"You don't get it!" she exploded.

"Try me."

"Look, you've got that perfect family—parents who love you, who support you no matter *what* you do. I mean, you're always sneaking around putting your nose into everything, half the town can't stand you for it—"

"Thanks?"

"—and your parents, they're like, whatever. They don't care. I mean, they even have your back."

"And yours don't?"

She glanced down at the carpet, rubbed her toe over a dime-size spot on the floor. "They're not horrible people or anything. They didn't, like, *abuse* me or anything like that. But they don't understand me."

I leaned forward in my chair. "Let me get this straight," I started, my voice trembling with repressed rage. "You staged your own kidnapping and set the whole town on a frantic manhunt because *your parents just don't understand you?*" I was practically spitting. "Melanie, my friend is actually missing! Do you get that?"

"See!" she said, tears welling in her eyes. "I knew you wouldn't get it! It's more than just, you know, stupid angst. I want to be an actress! Like for real, in the movies. And I think I have what it takes."

"Oh, I've seen you perform," I said. "But . . . you'd go to these lengths?"

"She's passionate," Anna added. She was seated next to Melanie at the edge of the twin bed, and she put a hand on her friend's shoulder now, comforting her.

"I want to go to acting school, out in California. But my parents want me to join my father's law firm."

"You're seventeen," I pointed out. And I had no time for her drama right now. "You have time to figure this stuff out without, I don't know, triggering an Amber Alert."

"They want me to go to school here in the northeast, come home on weekends to help out in the office, get exposed to it. I'm supposed to declare prelaw, and then I'm supposed to go to

Harvard Law after I graduate, just like my dad did, and join the firm as soon as I take the bar. He even knows which office will eventually be mine. It's all planned out."

"That sounds . . . stressful," I admitted. "But . . . this?" I looked around the room, watching dust motes catch in the few random spots of light that had woven their way in. "You couldn't have just talked to them?"

"She tried," Anna said. "Believe me."

"You have no idea how hard I tried," Melanie said. "It wasn't happening. And graduation is in a few months." She crossed her legs, shuffling back on the bed to get more comfortable. "I got into all the drama schools I applied to, you know. And I put a deposit down and everything. With my own savings, because I couldn't tell my parents about it. And then I got the letters from the schools *they* were looking at, the ones *they'd* forced me to apply to."

"You were rejected?" I asked.

"Of course not!" she sputtered. "That's the thing—I don't *get* rejected! I got into them all! And then *they* picked which one I was going to, like I wasn't even a person with thoughts or opinions of my own."

The anger and frustration I'd been feeling since I came in began to melt away, giving way to a fresh wave of urgency and fear for Daisy. Melanie's song was a variant on the poor-little-rich-girl refrain, sure, but that didn't mean it wasn't valid. This sounded rough. And as someone who *did* have parents in my corner every step of the way, like Melanie had said, I couldn't even imagine how she'd coped. It was amazing she hadn't snapped sooner.

"So you ran away," I offered.

"Well, that was the plan," she said. "As soon as that bird hit the window, I knew: This was my chance. Vanish, blame it on the curse, make it super dramatic and cinematic. I'd be Internet famous, and then resurface in LA free of my parents' judgment. Live my dream."

"Okay, I hear you. But it's still a *long* way to go for a little autonomy."

"Do you think they'd pay tuition if I didn't go to one of their schools? No, I had to make my own smoke and mirrors so that once I got out to California, I could support myself."

"Then why are you still *here*?" I asked. "There must be crappy motels between here and LA. Ones farther from home, where it would be way less likely for your parents to find you."

"Duh," she said. "But, yeah, that's the thing: I was only supposed to be here for a night. To regroup, you know? And then . . . I don't know, after that first night, it was harder than I expected to actually do it. To full-on take the plunge."

"You *need* to go home," I told her. "Whatever you may think about your parents, they're worried about you. And I'm sorry, but it's *really* screwing with the Naming Day investigations that your disappearance is tied up with them. I mean, you don't want to be even a little bit responsible for us never finding Daisy, right? And McGinnis could really use another witness to give information about the whole thing with the raven. . . ."

I trailed off, an image from my nightmares flashing in my head.

The wide-planked floor. The flapping of wings.

Obedience.

I gasped, standing up.

"I have to go," I said, short.

"Seriously?" Anna asked.

"Seriously," I said. "I just remembered something. Something important."

I sat in my car and pulled my phone out, my heart hammering. Quickly, I called up the photo I'd taken of the note Daisy's kidnappers left for Lena. It *looked* nondescript, sure . . . but I pinched at the screen, blowing the image up . . . until: There it was.

In the corner, torn.

A sliver of red.

The same shade as . . . a robin redbreast.

The pieces slid into place like a slot machine coming to rest.

Jackpot.

The raven.

My nightmare.

Daisy's mother, cold and haughty, wearing a robin scarf.

It made sense.

PART FOUR

THE RESCUE

These people, they cling to their hopes. To their facts. To their rational explanations. A curse? Never.

Even after an unexplainable float malfunction that left three high school students maimed for life, they still clung to facts.

Even after the year the lighthouse went up in flames.

Even after the year an unseasonable hurricane preempted the celebration and left the town hall in tatters.

Coincidence. Freak accident. Fluke. All of these episodes, these incidents, were waved away, explained easily enough. All of them could be easily connected to the known and real world.

But I'm here to remind them of the truth. To show them otherwise. To make clear that facts and explanations aren't the only things lurking in the shadows, here in Horseshoe Bay.

The girl will leave no stone unturned.

But she will soon believe.

CHAPTER TWENTY-ONE

The drive was twisty, the road unpaved for a good two miles before I even got up to the property. The land itself wouldn't have been found on any GPS system. If you didn't know about it, you wouldn't know about it.

But I knew.

It had been a long time since I'd been here, and I'd only been once, but I knew it.

I'd only needed the buzz of finding Melanie and her small nudge about the raven to *finally* jostle loose that memory that had been swirling around in the depths of my subconscious, taunting me.

OAKLAND GREEN. The sign was only there if you knew to look for it, the outline of an oak leaf etched into wood and nailed to a low tree trunk lining the edge of a rural road. This was the deep woods of Maine, well beyond Stone Ridge or even the summer camp territory.

This was where Daisy's family lived.

I'd been here once before—very young, one summer break, my parents packing a small bag for me and dropping me here so I could have a long weekend with Daisy on the family estate. Her mother used this farm for bird-watching, her favorite hobby. The estate was sprawling with buildings in varying states of dilapidation, many of which were off-limits to Daisy and me. Not that I particularly wanted to roam far beyond the main farmhouse— the trees surrounding the property were dense, meant to shield the Dewitts from the rest of the town, I realized later, and they were menacing.

Even when I was younger, before I'd honed my most keen detective instincts, I knew the Dewitts had secrets.

There were birds everywhere. Which seemed normal for a rural farm surrounded by forest, but as Daisy and I played on the wooden swing set in the backyard I couldn't stop myself from looking over my shoulder, on edge, thinking about where they could be hovering. Watching.

That night, during a summer lightning storm, an unkindness of ravens had become agitated, and they'd flapped and squawked and flailed against the window of the room where Daisy and I had rolled out our sleeping bags. While she'd slept soundly, I'd watched, frozen in fear as their wings rattled the glass, like something out of a Gothic horror story. And I'd never been a child who scared easily.

The next morning, it had all felt like a bad dream. At the breakfast table, Daisy was bright-eyed and chatty, mentioning nothing about a disturbance. I simply nodded and grimaced my way through my bowl of stale cornflakes.

And I never went back to the farm again.

Out of context, the memory seems innocuous enough—a bizarre brush with wildlife in a rural-adjacent Maine town isn't unheard-of. Not many people would make the connection to a note-bearing raven more than a decade later.

But I'm not just anyone.

CHAPTER TWENTY-TWO

The farmhouse came into view in the distance, on top of a hill, like something out of a scary movie. The original log cabin portion was over three hundred years old. It connected through a series of corridor additions to a stone house from the eighteen hundreds, and then a more "modern" wing of the traditional wooden saltbox style that still predated anyone in my own family's arrival in Maine by more than a few decades. Despite the incongruity of its components, the house itself felt solid, knowing—the saltbox windows like wide, piercing eyes standing guard, keeping close watch on any would-be trespassers.

Like me.

I pulled to the side of the path, searching for enough of a clearing in the woods that I could park but still be mostly hidden from view.

It was still bright out, daylight high. But I plucked my black knit beanie from the glove compartment and put it on anyway. It felt appropriate.

Now the question was: Why would the Dewitts go to such lengths to terrorize the school and the town? And worse, why would they make their own daughter disappear?

The log cabin was the oldest structure—and the one with the sturdiest cellar, originally used for storing food for winter, but retrofitted as a storm shelter. I remembered Daisy's uncle, who lived on the farm as well, showing the space to us. "This here'll keep you snug through Armageddon," he said.

Armageddon . . . or a kidnapping.

I was prepared for a series of obstacles, or at least elaborate locks. But when I got to the entrance to the cellar, it was just a regular old set of metal doors, the kind that opened like a book, held together with a chain, sure, but a chain clamped with a simple padlock.

I pulled out my lock-picking kit. *Don't leave home without it.*

My pick snapped, half of it breaking free and landing in my cupped palm like some injured insect.

Crap.

I grabbed my bag and rummaged through it, looking for something useful. *Aha!* A pot of lip gloss. I dug out a paper clip and scooped up a healthy dollop of the gloss, sliding the clip into the lock and jiggling it around until the broken half of the pick popped out.

Take two.

This time, the lock gave way immediately. *Note to self: There's a reason that people talk about "greasing the wheels."*

I pulled the doors apart, recoiling from the screech of rusty metal scraping against itself, bracing myself for what I'd find when I climbed down the ladder into the dank space.

"Daisy?!"

Somehow, improbably, a four-poster bed was down here, made up impeccably like something out of a fairy tale, which made the scene even more sinister. And there was Daisy—gaunt, pale, but otherwise intact, from what I could see—curled up in a ball, sleeping.

"Daisy!" I called again, more insistent this time.

She sat up with a start. "Nancy?" She blinked, disbelieving, but I could see when she fully registered that I was really there. Her eyes filled with tears. "We have to get out of here."

"So, let me get this straight," I said, after I'd had a few beats to process the fact that this was actually *Daisy*, right here before my eyes, not only fully intact and doing *fine* but apparently *not nearly as nonplussed about having been kidnapped by her whole family as I would have expected.* "You knew about this?"

"Not right away," she admitted. "I told you—how my parents were being so weird about the reenactment? Like they didn't want me to take part in it?"

"Um, yeah," I said, my head spinning. *"Daisy!"* The reality of her standing in front of me came over me again, overwhelming me, and I had to throw my arms around her, to touch her and know that she was here, that we were both really, actually here. Her perfume: still the tuberose. "I can't believe this."

"I know. Well, so, it turns out there *is* someone out there who knows about the Naming Day curse. A few someones . . ."

"And they're all related to me."

"Your *family* kidnapped you," I said. Even standing here, looking at her, it was almost impossible to fathom. "How? Did they hurt you?" Hot rage rose in me just thinking about it.

"No, I'm fine, I promise. Just . . . shaken. I think they, uh, drugged me," she said.

"*What?*"

"A sleeping pill, nothing dangerous," she said, waving it off. I didn't buy that wave one bit, but now wasn't the time to press her. She'd need all kinds of support from me just as soon as I got us out of here safely.

"*What?!*" I stared at her. "Daisy, that's *crazy* dangerous! How can you—? Wait, tell me later. Just—what is going on?"

"When it became clear that I wasn't going to quit the reenactment, like, even after the raven and that message in the grass, I guess they came up with plan B. And they took me here. It's not that bad, except for the total lack of Internet. And I guess it'll be over soon. It was . . . well, it was never supposed to go this far. I don't *think*." Her voice wavered, and I knew she was just barely holding it together.

"Daisy," I said, horror in my voice, "the minute *your own family drugged you*, it officially went too far." I looked around. "It's over *now*. Who's here with you?"

"Just my uncle," she said. "I think my parents are back in Horseshoe Bay, keeping up appearances."

"Right." The town hall meeting. I thought back to Mrs. Dewitt's performance. She was truly a pro; she should've been the one heading out to Hollywood to try her luck at a movie career instead of Melanie.

I looked at my phone. One bar. Daisy was right about the lack of Internet or any other kind of connectivity. Still, I texted 911 and tried to drop a pin for my parents, Lena, and Parker, just in case.

"We're getting out of here," I said.

I grabbed Daisy by the wrist and led her toward the cellar doors, still flung open. She scrambled up, and I followed.

I stepped out into the sunlight, then froze, hearing a twig crack behind me.

Then everything went black.

CHAPTER TWENTY-THREE

I woke with a headache and my wrists tied behind me.

"What's going on?" My tongue felt thick and fuzzy in my mouth.

"We did not escape," Daisy said simply. Her voice was eerily removed in a way that made me realize I'd need to be more than sharp enough for the both of us. I turned to my left, where her voice had come from, realizing that the throbbing in my head worsened when I moved it. She, too, was tied to a chair—one of the straight-backed, antique kitchen chairs from the stone house that, impossibly, I remembered from the sleepover.

The room was dark enough that I couldn't quite see where we were or who was with us . . . but I could feel a presence, and I could hazard a guess.

"Uncle Horton?"

"Present and accounted for."

A slim, spidery figure crept from a shadow, holding a kerosene lantern. The glow from the lamp made his gaunt cheekbones even more hollow, so that it appeared a ghoul or a phantom loomed over us.

Quickly, I took in the details of our surroundings:

Bound to a chair.

No window.

One door.

Daisy.

Horton.

I wiggled my wrists again the rope. No give.

"What the hell are you doing?" I demanded, trying to keep my voice even despite the thudding of my heart in my chest. I remembered Daisy saying it was never supposed to go too far. Famous last words.

"Oh, sweetie, you were always too suspicious for your own good," Horton said. "We never did think you were a great friend for Daisy."

"'We'?"

From out of the shadows, a group of people came forward, each holding a lantern of their own. *Time to readjust that assessment of your surroundings.*

I didn't recognize them all . . . but I *did* see Daisy's parents, front and center. So they weren't still in Horseshoe Bay. Coincidence, or did they know I was close to figuring everything out?

Mrs. Dewitt was wearing yet another one of her bird scarves, I realized with dawning horror.

"I guess if anyone would know about the Naming Day curse, it would be this family," I said.

"The Naming Day curse, yes," Mr. Dewitt began, clearing his throat like a he was about to deliver a Shakespearian monologue. "Local lore—obscure though it may be, and not by accident—says that a group of youths from the first settled colony went missing without a trace. But what's always left out of the tale is that the man who was meant to have caused the disappearance—"

"He was a Dewitt," I said, without missing a beat. *Of course.* It all made sense. I could see all too well now why Daisy's family wouldn't want her to participate in that.

"Exactly. Jonathan was wrongly persecuted. He was *innocent.*" Mr. Dewitt's features were warped with fury, and he seemed unable to go on.

Mrs. Dewitt stepped in. "And thus, we have our own cross to bear, and a curse of our own. When the Naming Day Festival was reestablished, we Dewitts supported it. We had to, to maintain our standing in the community, such that it was. But over time, tragedy followed that accursed celebration. And any year that a Dewitt got near a reenactment, devastation ensued. A Dewitt may not participate in the show."

"That's the curse?" A shiver went down my spine. Though there could have been correlation, there was no way what the Dewitts were saying could actually be attributed to anything beyond the real, physical world. All of this—it was all just a product of how bitterness warped and twisted the family. And that was just as frightening. "And your family was powerful enough to remove any mention of it in our town records or history?"

"My dear"—Mrs. Dewitt gave me a chilling smile that showed no teeth—"you have no idea how powerful we are."

Oh, I had some idea. These were people who thought curses were real. Who probably wouldn't have balked at the image I'd seen in my rearview mirror.

"I get it now," I said. "You removed any trace of the curse in the town records. Meanwhile, Dewitts' participation in the reenactment was rare enough and inconsistent enough that no one else ever realized what exactly the 'curse' was."

"No wonder you're known as the girl detective," Mr. Dewitt said. "Correct . . . and eventually, it became just another urban legend. Mostly buried."

"Why didn't you tell me, though?" Daisy asked.

"We keep the details of the curse *buried*," Horton reiterated through clenched teeth. "It's the only reason we've managed to pull ourselves out from infamy as much as we have. But given the stakes, we thought invoking it might yield quicker results, and no one would have been the wiser. If it weren't for *you*, Miss Drew." The venom in his voice nearly made me shiver, but I was able to meet his gaze.

"I would've understood," Daisy insisted. A tear slid down her cheek. "I wouldn't have auditioned. This is . . . insane. You've got me *fake-kidnapped*."

I shimmied in my seat, reflexively trying to raise my hand despite the fact that it was bound. "And me *real*-kidnapped." Daisy was way more generous than me. But maybe that was because in her case, it was family.

"You think you would have understood, child," her mother crooned, "but I know better. Your generation is so cynical. . . . You don't believe in superstitions, or curses."

"I mean, I'm beginning to be persuaded," I said, thinking of those dangling legs and trying to push the image from my mind. "Not in the magical side of things, though. If there's a Naming Day curse, it's been caused by your whacked-out behavior."

"Believe what you will," Mrs. Dewitt said, giving me a scathing look. "But if my sweet Daisy going missing wasn't enough to get the town to cancel Naming Day, maybe yet another disappearance will do the trick." She narrowed her eyes at me. "Or maybe we need to come up with a more . . . permanent solution for you."

Daisy was crying in earnest now, deep sobs that sent her chest straining against the ropes that bound her to the chair.

The air was filled, suddenly, with the sound of birds squawking. I looked at Daisy. "What's going on?"

The sound of wings flapping . . . the incessant beating rhythm from my nightmares . . . it rose up around us, pressing in from all sides, until it felt like it was coming from inside my body.

"Something's coming," Daisy said.

I cocked my head, concentrating. Slowly, I realized that beneath the sound of the frantic birds, I heard something else.

Something that made me smile.

My arms were still tightly bound behind me, thick twine biting into my wrists.

But my ankles were starting to come loose.

CHAPTER TWENTY-FOUR

One thing that good old Uncle Horton hadn't realized when he was tying Daisy and me up, apparently, was just how close he'd left one of his lanterns to my chair. And how loosely he'd bound my legs.

I flexed an ankle, testing a theory.

I turned to Daisy. "Be ready to follow my lead."

"What?"

I strained with my ankle, reaching—

And knocked the lamp over, sending glass shattering and a lick of flames along the wall.

The Dewitts began to shriek, immediately panicking and running in different directions like . . . well, "chickens with their heads cut off" was the obvious metaphor, but given the circumstances, I was more inclined to compare them to ravens.

"Daisy!" Mrs. Dewitt's eyes were wild, panicked.

"Don't worry!" I said. "I've got her." I held up my hands, now free, and quickly untied my legs, rushing to Daisy to untie her ropes too.

"How the hell did you . . . ?" Daisy started.

I cut her off. "I'm resourceful." I grabbed her hand. "We have to get out of here."

"I can't just leave them. . . ." She glanced at her family. "I know, they're monsters, but still."

"We're not leaving them." I paused, giving her a minute to take in the sound that had been steadily rising in the distance.

Finally, her face lit up as she realized. "Sirens."

I nodded. "It turns out, one bar was enough." I held out a hand. "You ready now?"

"Yes, *please*."

We ran.

EPILOGUE

can't believe instead of starring in the reenactment, I'm stuck here."

Daisy frowned at Lena and me from her hospital bed.

The fire department had arrived shortly after I'd sprung Daisy and me from our ties, and we'd escaped the farm without anyone getting seriously hurt. The Dewitts were down at the police department with McGinnis and Karen, being questioned. My father, who'd met Daisy's and my ambulance at the hospital on Karen's tip, assured me they'd probably be there for a while. In a way, it was ironic: In the end, the Dewitts got what they wanted. Naming Day was off.

Somehow, I didn't think it was quite the happy ending they'd been hoping for, though. And I doubted the celebration was off for good, either. Even if the Dewitts wouldn't be able to hold their secrets so tightly for very much longer. And their insistence of Jonathan's innocence—which lined up with Glynnis's suspicions about a scapegoat—nagged at me. Who was guilty, then? An unsolved mystery, likely never to *be* solved. But at least my friend was safe.

I turned my attention back to Daisy. "It's just for one night, for observation," I said. "You were held captive. You were drugged. I'm kind of okay with an abundance of caution."

"Easy for you to say." She sniffed. "You're footloose and fancy-free."

"Not quite," I said. "I still have to go down to the station tomorrow with my parents to give an official statement about what went down at the farm. And I have a feeling my parents are gonna be *very* attentive for at least the next few days."

Dad had made it clear that concern for my well-being trumped any anger over my putting myself in danger to investigate Daisy. But that didn't mean that anger, too, wasn't still layered in there, waiting until the initial shock of the ordeal had worn off.

It was going to be a long weekend. But I didn't mind—too much. Daisy was back, safe. The mystery was put to bed. Life was pretty good, all things considered.

"Special delivery!" A giant bouquet of balloons appeared in the doorway.

"Daisy, your boyfriend's legs have arrived. With the balloons from *Up*, apparently," Lena said.

"Don't be jelly," Daisy said, blushing with pleasure as Cooper wrangled the arrangement into the room and quickly crossed to her bedside.

"Here," Lena said, taking out her phone. "We can revisit the glory of Naming Day through my masterful social media campaign."

She passed the phone to Daisy, who scrolled through, a small nostalgic smile crossing her face. She squealed. "Oh, remember this one? *My best friends are starving!*"

"I remember waiting for almost an hour for an order of cheese fries," Lena said.

"Let me see." I reached for the phone. Friday—one week ago, which felt more like five months. There we were, beaming away, with no idea what Naming Day would have in store for us. "We were such innocent babes in the woods."

"Well, at the beach," Daisy corrected.

"Though I did have a brief detour to the woods," I reminded her. "For sleuthing purposes."

I blinked. For a second, it seemed like the phone screen shimmered. I squinted.

There, in the picture, hovering over my head . . .

A face. Faint, but there. Gaunt and scared. But angry, too.

I blinked, and it was gone. It was just a shot of the three of us again—Lena, Daisy, and me, hopeful and bright and eager for whatever Naming Day would bring.

"Nancy?" Daisy asked, uncertain. "You look like you've seen a ghost."

Definitely not. "Just delusions born from exhaustion." I passed the phone back to Lena. "It's nothing."

* * *

The town square pagoda had a very different feel to it tonight, with the (thankfully, finally canceled) Naming Day Festival behind it, with most people home, reveling in the peace and quiet that had fallen over Horseshoe Bay, *finally*, in the wake of Daisy's and Melanie's (and, evidently, my own) disappearances being cleared up.

And with Parker by my side, from the onset, as opposed to lingering shadows and tiny jump scares lying in wait, remnants of my own subconscious trying to jolt me into memories I'd long since packed away.

At least, that was the story I was telling myself about the images I'd seen, those eerie moments that were still, somehow, unexplainable, even with the rest of the "curse" having been dragged out into the open and cut apart, neatly dissected and rationally explained.

"I can't believe it turned out that Daisy's own parents were behind the curse stuff," Parker said. "Kidnapping their *own* daughter. Do you think Daisy was in on it?"

I leaned against his chest, liking the warmth. "I don't know. Denial is a pretty powerful force. Maybe some part of her had an idea. She *did* say they were being weird, when she first was cast. And she didn't want me to go to the principal when the raven hit the window."

"Does that make her *more* likely to have been in on it, or less?"

"She had to know. It was a *raven*. And I guess she thought . . . if we didn't tell anyone, and things just went on, business as usual . . .

that they'd have to give up and put their whole curse thing aside."

"That was wildly optimistic of her."

"Yeah, she definitely underestimated her family's commitment to the whole Naming-Day-curse thing." I snuggled closer, sliding my arms around him. "If it's any consolation, I think the whole kidnapping-her-and-then-threatening-to-kill-her-best-friend thing really made it clear."

"Good," Parker said, kissing me on the forehead. "Except I wish it hadn't come to that."

"Me too. Seeing as how it was me they were threatening to kill."

Parker sat up, jostling me. He put his hands on my shoulders, looking searchingly into my eyes. "I get it. You're a badass. And it's hot, and you're smart, and so strong. But seriously, Nancy—that was *dangerous*. And you're just . . . I don't know, *joking* about it?"

"I single-handedly rescued myself and one of my best friends from dangerous kidnappers," I said. "I think I've earned the right to joke about it if I want to."

"Dating you is going to drive me to an early grave."

I gave him a slow smile, trying to cajole him. "So you're saying you want to be dating me?"

"Despite what it's doing to my stress levels, yes," he said.

"Excellent," I said. "Now that the mystery of the ancient curse has been solved, things should be pretty quiet. Perfect circumstances for a burgeoning romance."

He kissed me, slow and deep. My toes curled in my shoes. It was a kiss that managed to subdue the lingering questions I was having about Parker, and about what his quaint tendency toward "concern" could mean for any future mysteries that might arise.

Because mysteries *always* seemed to arise. Even when I wasn't looking for them.

I thought the girl would bring the truth to light. But in the end, her loyalty to her friend, her love for tidy, earthly explanations . . . it overrode all other aspects of the legend, of the need to bring the town's sordid history to light.

For now.

And I can accept that.

For now.

My spirit has lingered this long; she will surely find a way to bide her time until the next moment, the opportunity for revenge, is upon us.

About the Author

Micol Ostow has written over fifty works for readers of all ages, including projects based on properties like *Buffy the Vampire Slayer*, *Charmed*, and *Mean Girls*. In addition to *Nancy Drew*, she currently writes the bestselling *Riverdale* novels and comics based on the original Archie Comics characters. She lives in Brooklyn with her husband, two daughters, piles and piles of books, and all the streaming channels. In her past life, she may have been a teen sleuth. Visit Micol online at MicolOstow.com.